JoGo - Do you not know that in a
race, all the runners run, but only
one wins the prize? Run in such
a way as to win the prize!

1 Cor. 9:24

Many blessings!

Chop, Chop

Book One

L.N. Cronk

Front Cover Photography by Inga Ivanova.
Back Cover Photography by Nautilus Shell Studios (top)
and French Knob Ventures (bottom).

Spanish translations provided by Vicki Oliver Krueger.

Scripture taken from the HOLY BIBLE, NEW INTERNATIONAL
VERSION ®. Copyright © 1973, 1978, 1984 by International Bible
Society. Used by permission of Zondervan. All rights reserved.

This book is a work of fiction. Names, characters, places and
incidents are products of the author's imagination or are used
fictitiously. Any resemblance to actual events or locales or persons,
living or dead, is entirely coincidental.

ISBN Number: 978-0-9820027-0-4
Library of Congress Control Number: 2008933006

Published by Rivulet Publishing
West Jefferson, NC, 28694, U.S.A.

For my 8th Grade Geometry Class.

I have fought the good fight, I have finished the race, I have kept the faith. - 2 Timothy 4:7

~ ~ ~

HE'S GOING TO be the youngest person executed in our state since the death penalty was reinstated in 1975. Men, women, and even a few children line the driveway leading to the gate of the compound. Flickering candlelight illuminates their sad or angry faces. They wave their signs and occasionally pound on the windows of our car, as if they are angry with us. I wonder briefly why they're mad at us when they don't even know why we're here.

I am squashed in the middle of the back seat with Laci on one side and our old Sunday school teacher on the other — not old as in aged, but old as in she's not my Sunday school teacher anymore. It's because of her that Laci and I are here, attending our first execution.

I peer ahead as the gates swing open to let us through. There was a time when I hardly ever cried, but now it seems like anything can set me off and the tears start to slide down my face again. I'm not embarrassed anymore because they've both seen me cry more than I care to admit. Laci reaches over and takes my hand. I lean my head back on the headrest and close my eyes.

~ ~ ~

TO TELL THIS story, I am going to have to start with Laci, and since it *starts* with me and Laci, and *ends* with me and Laci, you're probably going to think that it's a story *about* me and Laci. But you're wrong . . . it's not. Not really. But I can't just jump into what the story *is* about. I have to start at the beginning, and that does mean starting with Laci.

I've known her ever since we were in preschool and I remember hiding under the stairs with her and tasting Play-Doh. I realize that this sounds disgusting, but I'm going to have to be completely honest with you if anything good is going to come out of recalling this story. Telling this story is the most difficult thing I've ever had to do, and if nothing good is going to come of it, then I'd just as soon not go through with it at all.

Anyway, I remember hiding under the stairs and tasting Play-Doh with Laci. If you ask most grown-ups, they'll admit to tasting it too. That makes it especially disgusting when you think how many other kids had probably tasted it before we got to it, but for some reason, this is my earliest memory of me and Laci together.

Laci was (and still is) very pretty. I think I have probably always realized this, even before I was old enough to be interested in girls, but Laci has never been worried about her looks. Instead, Laci has always worried about other people.

When she was four years old, her mother was watching a talk show on TV and it featured people who were cutting their hair off and sending it to Locks of Love to be made into wigs for children who – for various medical reasons – did not have any hair. Four-year-old Laci apparently took one look at a little girl on that show who had no hair, made the giant mental leap that she could help, and insisted that her mother help her cut off her long, pretty, brown hair so that they could send it to Locks of Love. She still has the little thank-you card that they sent her in return.

I don't remember any of this, but I'm told that the next day she showed up at preschool and I thought we had a new boy in class. When Mom picked me up that afternoon the preschool teacher told her, "*David really freaked out today . . .*"

Apparently, even after the teacher calmed me down, I refused to have anything to do with Laci and I never hid under the stairs with her and tasted Play-Doh again. Like I said, I have no memory of this, but my mother thinks the story is quite funny and she's told it so many times that I figure it must be true.

I do remember though, in the second grade, telling Laci that I liked her hair long. She had grown it back and it was cascading down past her shoulder blades. She smiled at me and said "Thank you, David," but apparently she didn't care too much what I thought because she whacked it all off again a few weeks later. Evidently, Laci thought that her head was a hair farm.

It had grown out long again by the time we were in the fifth grade. In addition to preschool and elementary school, Laci and I went to church together too. One day, in Sunday school, our teacher was talking to us about the importance of giving. One of the students said that what Laci was doing – growing her hair out and donating it – was another way of giving to others. The teacher thought this was an excellent point, but I didn't agree.

"Why on *earth* not, David?" the teacher wanted to know.

"Because," I explained, "it says in the Bible that when you give to the needy you're not even supposed to let your left hand know what your right hand is doing . . . you're supposed to give in secret." The teacher looked surprised. She probably thought I never paid attention during lessons.

"You're only supposed to let *God* know what you're doing," I went on. "*Everybody* knows what she's doing."

"Well, I suppose that technically you're correct, David," the teacher said, "but what Laci's doing is kind and very giving and there's really no way for her to do it in secret."

"That's not true," I argued. "She doesn't have to cut it so short and make herself look like a *boy*. She just does that so everyone will know that she's giving it to Locks of Love.

"She could get her hair cut shorter in a way that looks *nice*," and I glared at her as I emphasized the word nice, "and then people would just think that she's had a haircut. No one would even have to know what she did with it after it was all cut off."

I don't remember what the teacher said to me, but I do remember that Laci looked down at her hands which were folded in her lap. I felt a little twinge of guilt (but not much) and for some reason I felt quite proud of myself when she came to school a few months later with her hair in a short, but feminine, bob.

By the time Greg arrived in town, Laci and I were pretty much friends. I don't mean that we hung around together or anything, but we saw each other all the time – either in class or church or something – and I figured she had forgiven me for freaking out in preschool and for being mean to her in the fifth grade. One time I even thought she might have been flirting with me when she asked me to help her with her locker because it popped right open on my first try.

I told myself it was probably just a lucky break.

It was the summer before seventh grade when Greg moved to our neighborhood and Laci's hair was at stage two. (Somewhere along the way I had developed my own private system for assessing what phase Laci's hair was at in the "grow it out and chop it off" cycle. Stage one is when it's so short that she can't even get it into a ponytail. Stage two is when it hits her shoulders. Stage three is when it's long and you know she's about to get it cut off again.)

But back to Greg...

When I first saw Greg, it never occurred to me that I was looking at someone who was going to become the best friend I would ever have. I've never been the most social person in the world anyway and I already had two great friends ... Mike and Tanner. I figured that was pretty much all I needed.

Like Laci, I had known Mike and Tanner for most of my life. Mike also went to the same church, but was a grade below me, and Tanner was in the same grade as me, but went to a different church. In just one year, Mike would be at the junior high school too, and until then we had soccer and basketball and baseball and Scouts and summers at the pool.

It was at the pool that I first saw Greg. We had just finished swimming and Tanner had taken his youngest brother, Jordan, to the kiddy pool. Mike and I were drying off on the concrete, waiting for him. Neither one of us was going to get into the kiddy pool with them because (even though we didn't have little brothers or sisters ourselves) we knew enough not to trust the swimmy diapers that the little kids all wear. When Tanner finally convinced his mom to take over watching Jordan, he joined us in the sun.

"Hey, Dave!" he said to me. "See that guy over there?" Tanner nodded toward the kiddy pool. Mike and I both sat up on our elbows and looked.

"What about him?" I asked.

"His name's Greg. He's new here. His family just moved to Cavendish from Florida. He's going to be in the seventh grade this fall too."

"Lucky," Mike muttered, lying back down.

"Oh quit whining," I told Mike. "I'd gladly stay in the sixth grade."

"Not all by yourself you wouldn't!"

"Oh, yes I would!" I said. "You're the one who's lucky. We're going to have eighth graders stuffing our heads into toilets and filling our lockers with syrup and hours of homework every night . . ."

"It's not gonna to be like that!" Tanner argued.

"Yeah, I know. I was just trying to make Mikey feel better."

"Thanks a lot," Mike said.

"No problem."

I looked at the new kid again. He was playing with Jordan and a little girl. I hoped for his sake that the little girl was his sister – that was the *only* excuse someone his age had for hanging out in the kiddy pool.

"We should try to be nice to him," Tanner continued, still looking at me.

"Well I wasn't planning on being *mean* to him," I said.

"I know, but I just meant . . . well . . ." Tanner seemed unsure how to word what he wanted to say. "I just feel sorry for him, that's all. It's got to be hard moving to a new place and starting junior high school without any friends."

"Nobody's worrying about me starting sixth grade without any friends," Mike said.

"Oh, stop it!" Tanner said, hitting him with the back of his hand. "You've known everybody in your grade since you were in kindergarten."

"Preschool," I corrected him.

"Anyway," Tanner continued, "I was just thinking how I would feel if I were him and I thought maybe . . ."

"Sure," I agreed. "We can save a spot for him at the lunch table, and I'll share my locker with him, and you can carry his books for him on the way home from school and–"

"Oh shut up," Tanner said, smacking me this time. But he had a big grin on his face and I could tell he knew that I was going to be nice to the new kid.

Nobody, it turned out, needed to worry about the new kid. Greg would have been fine without any extra niceness from me or Tanner or anyone else. The next time I saw him was at church the following Sunday. The entire congregation was murmuring about the arrival of a new family. After church, Mike and I were standing against his mom's car talking when Greg walked up to us, carrying the little girl we'd seen him playing with in the pool.

"Hi!" he said, extending his hand. "I'm Greg White. This is my sister, Charlotte."

"Hi," I said, looking at his hand. Rising seventh graders didn't shake hands with each other.

"I'm Mike!" Mike said, sticking his hand into Greg's and pumping it up and down.

"I'm David," I said, hesitantly sticking my hand out. Greg shook it and Charlotte eyed me suspiciously.

"Listen," he went on. "My dad's going to be leading a new youth fellowship group. It's for junior high school students. I wanted to invite both of you to come."

Here he was, the new kid – the one who was supposed to be feeling awkward and lonely – but he was inviting *us* to something.

"I'm only going to be in the sixth grade," Mike said glumly. (Mike was kind of big for his age.)

"Oh," Greg said as a woman approached us.

"Do you want me to take Charlotte?" she asked Greg.

"No," he said, "she's fine. Mom, this is Mike and this is David."

She looked at us and smiled. Mike stuck out his hand and for some reason I felt like smacking him. She shook both of our hands.

"So nice to meet both of you!" she said. "I'm sure you boys are going to enjoy getting to know one another. Did Greg tell you? My husband is going to be leading a new youth fellowship group. I hope you'll both consider joining."

"I can't," Mike said, "I'm only going to be in the sixth grade."

"Oh, what a shame. Well, next year maybe?"

Mike nodded as she turned her eyes to me.

"What grade will you be in David?"

"Seventh."

"Oh! Wonderful! You and Greg will probably have some classes together . . ."

I nodded.

"Da-da!" Charlotte said, pointing in the direction of a man who was talking with my parents near the church steps.

"You want to go see Daddy?" Greg asked her. He looked at Mike and me before leaving. "I'll be seeing you guys around, okay?"

"See ya."

"Bye."

We watched them walk toward my parents and Greg put Charlotte down on the ground so she could waddle over to her father.

"What do you think?" Mike asked.

"I think he's lucky Tanner talked us into being nice to him. Obviously he's going to have a hard time making friends."

"Really?"

"No, not really you moron. I was being sarcastic."

"Oh," Mike said. "Are you going to join the youth group?"

"Well, look at them all over there talking . . . what do you think?"

We watched Greg and Greg's parents talking with my parents and we saw my mom lean down to pick up Charlotte.

"I think your mom's going to make you join youth group whether you want to or not!" he said, laughing at me.

"See?" I told him. "Being in the sixth grade might not be so bad after all."

What actually turned out to not be so bad after all was the new youth group, which started up two weeks later. During the first few weeks after I met Greg I was (for the *briefest* amount of time) slightly resentful of him. Now remember that I am trying to be completely honest here. Besides, who wouldn't be just *slightly* resentful if some new guy moved to their hometown and was soon hanging out at the pool every day showing their best friends how to turn flips off the high dive? And after church in the fellowship hall, I walked past just in time to see Laci dunk his head into the water fountain as he got a drink. He splashed her with water and she squealed. I really couldn't have cared less if she flirted with him, but it was a little discouraging to think that in just three weeks he'd pretty much landed in the same spot I'd spent twelve and a half years getting to.

Two weekends before school started, Mr. White took the youth group on a Saturday trip to Six Flags. By this time, I was over my *brief* and *slight* resentment of Greg. I couldn't put my finger on what it was that made everyone like him, but whatever it was, it worked on me too.

It was a three-hour trip each way so we had to leave at six in the morning. Nick's mom drove one car with our only three eighth graders (Matthew, Evan and Nick) and I rode in the White's van with the other seventh graders – Greg, Laci, Ashlyn and Natalie. Somehow I got stuck in the back with Laci. On the drive we listened to contemporary Christian music for the entire three hours. I'd never heard the songs before so I didn't join in as they held imaginary microphones to their mouths and crooned along.

"Come on, David!" Greg said, reaching back and pretending to stick a microphone in my face.

"I'm not singing," I said.

"Why not?"

"Because I don't want to."

"Is he always this grumpy?" Greg wanted to know. Laci and Ashlyn and Natalie all nodded.

"I am NOT grumpy!" I told them.

"Let me scoot over so I don't get struck by lightning," Laci said, moving away from me.

"What are you *talking* about?" I asked. "I'm not grumpy."

"Yes, you are," Natalie said and Ashlyn nodded.

"I'm a very HAPPY person!" I argued, and they all laughed.

"Yeah," Laci told Greg. "This is him at happy . . . watch out when he's mad."

"Now, now," Mr. White said from the front seat. "I don't think David's grumpy. Some people just aren't as . . . *jovial* as others, that's all."

"That's how we'll describe you from now on," Laci agreed. "*Non-jovial*."

"It's easier just to say that he's grumpy," Greg said.

"I've never seen anybody lose a tan so fast before," Greg was saying a few hours later. "You look really, really white."

I moaned.

When we'd arrived at the park, Mr. White had let us go off on our own and the girls separated from the boys. All the guys kept trying to convince me to ride a roller coaster with three loops on it, but I didn't want to go.

"Come on, David . . . don't be chicken," they'd said.

"I'm not chicken," I'd answered. "I get motion sickness."

I really did. My older sister Jessica had wound me up on a tire swing when I was four and I was so sick afterwards that Mom had taken me to the doctor.

But the guys didn't listen and hadn't given up . . .

Now we were sitting at a booth and Greg was eating a turkey leg and curly fries. I was a little put out with him for eating in front of me while I was so sick, but he'd been the only one that had stuck around while I was hanging over a trashcan for fifteen minutes so I couldn't really complain.

"Wanna fry?" Greg asked.

I moaned again.

"At least you're not wasting a lot of money on food," he said, and I put my head down on the table.

In about an hour I was feeling better, and by the time we got on the road to go home I was hungry. Mr. White pulled into a drive-thru for me and popped in an old CD while we were waiting for my food. As we pulled away, Ashlyn, who was sitting up front, started looking at the CD case.

"Hey, you guys," she said after a minute. "You know that song he sings . . . *Back in His Arms Again*?"

I didn't even know who *he* was, but everybody else was nodding.

"It says here that he wrote it because one of the kids that had been in his youth group came home from college over Christmas break all upset because he felt like he had gotten so far away from God . . ."

"I didn't know that," Laci said.

"Here," Ashlyn said, turning up the volume. "It's the next song."

Of course everybody else sang along while it played.

"I like it better if I know what a song is about when I hear it," Natalie said after it was over.

"Yeah," Laci agreed, "when I'm a DJ I'm going to share stuff like that with my listeners."

"*You're* going to be a DJ?" I asked skeptically.

She held up another fake microphone.

"That was the latest from Casting Crowns. Up next, a song from Mark Schultz and the story behind it, but first, let's check in with David in the weather center for an update on the storm that's been ravaging the Midwest . . . David?" She stuck her fake microphone in my face.

She'd actually sounded pretty impressive, but I rolled my eyes. I was just about to make a comment about her having a good face for radio when Greg pretended to grab her microphone and talk into it.

"I'm sorry, Laci, but David is indisposed at the moment. We regret to inform our listeners that he has a serious case of non-jovialness."

~ ~ ~

SEVENTH GRADE BROUGHT us kids from the south side of town together with the kids from the north. Until then we'd pretty much had our own churches, our own recreational leagues and our own community pools, so there truly were a lot of kids that we'd never met before.

The first one I wanted to get to know was Samantha. She sat in front of me in social studies and I didn't learn much that year in class. If teachers really want to improve test scores across the nation they should put the girls in the back of the classroom and the boys in the front. At least that way we'd have to blatantly turn right around in our seats to be distracted by the girls. When they're sitting right in front of us, we pretty much don't have a choice.

Samantha had dark hair, almost black, and it was long and straight and shiny and cut to the same length all around. I looked at it *a lot* because it was right in my face all during social studies and I found myself hoping that she wasn't going to get any big ideas from Laci about donating it – I liked her hair right where it was. She would lean over to pass notes to her best friend, Angel, and when she sat back up her hair would fall into perfect place as if it had just been brushed. Her hair wasn't the only thing about her that mesmerized me.

I didn't let on to anyone how fascinated I was with Samantha. Tanner had made the mistake of letting me and Mike know that he liked a girl named Calen in the sixth grade and we had teased him mercilessly and embarrassed him so badly that Calen would have nothing to do with him. It was probably fresh enough in Tanner's mind that payback would be certain and I wasn't going to do anything to mess up my relationship with Samantha.

Of course, I use the word "relationship" rather loosely here. My relationship with Sam consisted of me staring at her hair instead of

13

listening to Mrs. Harper's explanation of the major causes of World War II. When first quarter mid-term reports went home I really caught it from my mother at dinnertime.

"What in the *world* is going on in social studies?" she gasped when she saw my grade. "You've always done excellent in that class."

I shrugged. "I don't know . . . I just don't get it."

"What is there to '*get*'?" she wanted to know.

"The teacher just doesn't explain things good."

"Well," she corrected me.

"That either."

"I'm going to set up a conference . . ." she began.

"No! No! No! You don't have to do that. I promise I'll do better. Please! I promise! *Please* give me one more chance."

She frowned and glanced at my father before finally relenting.

"Last chance," she warned. "If you haven't brought this up by report card time you're not going to play basketball."

I think I was more afraid that she was going to talk to the teacher and I'd wind up with a new assigned seat than I was of not playing basketball. I dragged my social studies book home every night and studied enough to pull my grade up to a low A. It was a lot easier to understand the stuff at home anyway – when Sam and her hair weren't sitting in front of me.

Shortly after school started, our youth group had its first fundraiser. Mr. White had all sorts of great ideas lined up for the year, including a ski trip as soon as cold weather set in and an ice-fishing trip over a long weekend at the end of February. Although we lived in the cold Midwest, the nearest ski slopes were almost four hours away and I hardly ever got to go. I'd always wanted to go ice fishing too. Dad was an accountant and the winter months were the busiest for him. He took me fishing at Cross Lake every spring and summer after tax season was over, but I'd never been ice fishing before.

We held a Saturday car wash in the parking lot of a bank one block from our church and we earned over four hundred dollars. When we were finished, Laci's dad arrived to pick up Laci and Ashlyn.

"Need a ride, David?" he called out through Laci's open door. Laci lived just three blocks further from me than Greg did.

"Um . . ." I hesitated, not quite sure what to do. Mom was supposed to pick me up in about half of an hour. I kept telling her that if she'd buy me my own phone it could save her a lot of time.

"I'll give him a lift," Mr. White called out from behind me. Laci's dad waved and nodded and then pulled away.

"Guess I should have asked you what *you* wanted to do," Mr. White said as he coiled up a hose.

"No," I said, "that's fine, but I think my mom's supposed to be here in a little bit."

"No problem," he said, "that'll give us a chance to clean up while we're waiting."

It didn't take long to clean up and soon Greg and I were sitting on the curb waiting while Mr. White walked over to the church to run off some photocopies for the next night's youth group meeting.

"Sorry about that," Greg said after his dad had left.

"Sorry about what?"

"I figured you wanted to ride home with Laci."

"Huh?" I was totally lost.

"You know . . . *Laci!*"

"What about her?"

"I just figured you'd want to ride home with her and my dad kind of messed it up for you."

"Why would I want to ride home with Laci?"

"You know, I kind of thought that you liked her."

"*Laci?!*" I spluttered. "Why *on earth* would you think that I liked Laci?"

"She just seems like your type."

Maybe he hadn't noticed Sam yet.

"No," I said, "trust me. I didn't want to ride home with her."

"She's pretty . . ." he continued.

"Yeah, right now she is . . . but just wait."

Now it was his turn to be lost. I proceeded to tell him all about Laci and her hair and Locks of Love.

"That's pretty cool that she does that," Greg said when I had finished.

"I suppose . . ." I agreed somewhat reluctantly.

"We should do that."

"Do what?"

"You know . . . grow our hair out and donate it to Locks of Love."

I must have looked at him blankly.

"You know," he held out two fingers in a "V" and moved them together like scissors, cutting. "Chop, chop."

"*What?*"

"We should grow our hair out and donate it to—"

"Are you *CRAZY?!*"

"Nooo," he said, shaking his head and looking perplexed. "Why?"

"Because we're *BOYS* . . ."

"So?"

"*Soooo* . . . boys don't grow their hair long and donate it to Locks of Love!"

"Why not?"

"Because," I said again, "we're *BOYS!*"

He waved his hand at me as if he were dismissing me. "A lot of guys wear their hair long."

"Not *that* long!" I argued.

16

"Sure they do," he said and then he shrugged. "I think it's a good idea."

"You're crazy."

"No, I'm not," he said, moving his fingers like scissors again. "Chop, chop!"

And that was the start of Greg's hand signals.

Greg's hand signals went far beyond the thumbs up for "good job", or the okay symbol, or even twisting an imaginary sharpener around a pencil to see if you had one to loan him during a quiz. Every hand signal that Greg thought up *meant* something. Something funny or something that was important or something that he wanted you to think about.

I didn't understand that right away. For the next couple of months he'd catch my eye in science class and give me the "chop, chop" signal. I usually just waved him away or shook my head. Sometimes I gave him the universal "you're crazy" sign by twirling my finger around the side of my head, but I'd had two haircuts since our talk on the curb when I finally noticed that his hair was curling down over his ears and touching the collar on the back of his shirt.

"You aren't really going to let your hair get that long, are you?" I asked him at lunch.

"Yes, I am," he said matter-of-factly.

"Oh, boy," I replied. "You're really losing it, you know that?"

"No I'm not," he said, shaking his head. "You should do it too."

Chop, chop.

Sometime during soccer season, Greg's mom and my mom figured out that it would save them both a lot of time if one of them picked us up from soccer on Wednesdays, fed us both dinner, and then took us to youth group. The first Wednesday we did this, Mrs. White picked us up.

"Do you like lasagna?" she asked me as soon as we got in the car. Greg sat in the back with Charlotte, who was strapped in her car seat, and I sat in the front next to Mrs. White.

"I *love* lasagna," I said. I would have told her I loved liver and onions if she'd asked because my mom had been harping on me for three days about minding my manners, but I really did love lasagna and practice had left me hungry.

"Don't worry, Mom," Greg said. "David'll eat anything."

"I will *not!*"

"You eat that school pizza almost every day!"

"It's good!" I protested.

"See, Mom," Greg continued, "if he thinks the school pizza's good, he's going to think your lasagna's fantastic."

"You don't think my lasagna's fantastic?" she asked him.

"Well . . . I think it's better than the school pizza . . ."

She glanced at me.

"Would you please hit him for me?" she asked.

"Gladly!" I turned around and punched him in the leg.

"Hey!" he said, trying to hit me back, but not being quite quick enough. Charlotte squealed with delight.

We pulled into the drive and I helped Charlotte get out of her car seat and I held her hand as we walked up to the front door because Mom had told me to be helpful. Charlotte wanted to ring the doorbell and Mrs. White said that would be fine so I held her up and let her press the white button. Mr. White answered the door.

"Hello, David!" he said, taking Charlotte from me.

"Hi."

"You boys wash up right away," Mrs. White said as she scooted past us and walked toward the kitchen, "we don't have a lot of time before youth group."

She didn't have to tell me twice. I was *starving*.

When we sat down at the table, Charlotte reached down from her high chair and grabbed at my hand. I was thinking how cute it was that she wanted to hold my hand again, but then I realized that Greg was reaching for my other hand and that Mr. White was reaching across the table for Charlotte's free hand and that she had already put her little head down to pray.

"Thank you, Father," Mr. White began, "for bringing us together this evening. We especially thank You that David is here with us and we ask Your special blessing on him this evening."

I was already uncomfortable because I was holding hands with Greg, but having Mr. White pray for me was almost painful.

"I ask that You be with each of the young people who will be with us this evening and that You prepare their hearts and minds for fellowship with each other and with You."

Then Mrs. White prayed.

"Lord, I thank You for this day and for the many gifts You have given us. I especially ask that You will give me patience as I try to teach Charlotte about You every day and that You will guide me every moment as I take care of her."

I panicked when Greg started praying too because I knew for sure now that we were going clockwise and that I was going to be next.

I didn't catch one thing that Greg said.

19

When he was done I said, "Lord, we thank You for this food that You have provided for us. Please bless this food to our use and us to Your service."

That was exactly what my dad said *every* night at our dinner table and nobody gasped in horror so I figured I'd done alright. Charlotte said "Amen" and we all dropped hands.

The lasagna was fantastic.

The next night at the table Dad said our usual grace and had his fork in his hand before I could even say what had been on my mind.

"Um . . . I think we should say something else . . ."

"Something else?" Dad looked at me blankly.

"Uh . . . yeah, you know, something more . . . like . . . um . . ." I glanced at Mom for help, but she had the same blank look on her face.

"I just think that God would probably like to hear something a little more interesting than the same thing every day, and I thought that maybe," I cleared my throat, "we could, like, each say something different."

It probably didn't take any of them too long to figure out where the sudden inspiration for my suggestion had come from.

Mom finally spoke. "Okay, David, that would be nice. Why don't you start?"

I'd been thinking about it all day, so I was ready to go.

"Dear Lord, I thank You that we are all here together and that I did so well on my social studies test yesterday." (I figured it wouldn't hurt for Mom to hear that too, and besides, I really was thankful for it.)

"Well," Mom began, "I'm also thankful that David did well on his social studies test . . . and I thank You for this lovely home that You have provided for us."

20

After a moment of silence Jessica spoke. "I'm thankful for my family and my friends."

I couldn't help but feel a little sorry for Dad. I had my head bowed, but I heard him put down his fork.

"Thank You, Lord, for the many blessings You have given us. Thank You for my lovely wife and the wonderful meals she cooks for us. Thank You for Jessica and David. Please continue to bless this family."

I decided that I hadn't given him enough credit, and when I looked up, I saw Mom smiling at him.

I'm not sure exactly why I wanted us to pray at dinner that night the way the White's had. Maybe I didn't want to be embarrassed the following week when Greg came to our house, but maybe I knew that God deserved something more than we'd been giving Him. By the time Greg came to dinner the next week most of the awkwardness was gone. We might not have held hands, but even after soccer season ended we were still doing it.

~ ~ ~

IN NOVEMBER, THE PTO announced that they would be hosting a dance in the gym. I really wanted to ask Samantha to go, but I didn't dare. I'd been sitting behind her in social studies for almost four months and we'd barely spoken. I wasn't even positive that she knew my name.

Basketball tryouts were going on all week. While Tanner's group was out on the floor doing lay-ups, the group that Greg and I were in watched from the bleachers.

"Are you going to the dance?" he asked me.

"I doubt it," I said.

"You should ask someone," he encouraged.

I just shook my head.

"Oh, come on. If you were going to ask someone, who would it be?"

"I'm not sure . . ." I lied.

"Yeah, right!"

"Okay, then . . . who would you ask?" I demanded.

"You tell me first."

I hesitated for a few moments and then finally said, "*Promise* you won't tell anyone?"

He nodded his head and I believed him.

I leaned my head toward his and whispered, even though no one was sitting close to us. "Samantha!"

A look of surprise crossed his face.

"What's the matter with her?" I asked, defensively.

"Nothing's wrong with her . . . I just didn't know that you liked her."

"*No one* knows I like her and it had better stay that way!"

"I promised you I wouldn't tell anyone," he said.

"What about you?" I asked.

"Thank you, but I don't dance very well . . . you'd be better off asking someone else," he grinned.

"Oh, come on . . . you promised you'd tell me. Who would you ask?"

"You mean who *did* I ask!"

"You already asked someone?"

He nodded.

I was impressed. Maybe I should invite Samantha after all.

"Who?"

"Laci."

"You and Laci are going to the dance?" This didn't surprise me; ever since the carwash it had seemed to me as if they'd been spending a *lot* of time together.

"No," he said. "She doesn't want to go with me."

That *did* surprise me, but it also reaffirmed my decision to not ask Sam – there was too much danger of being shot down.

"Why not?"

"She likes somebody else."

"Oh," I said, unsure what to say.

"It's okay," he said. "We're still friends."

"Well," I said, sighing, "that's a lot more than I am with Sam."

We left on the first day of winter break to go skiing. The lodge was supposed to look rustic, but it was the nicest place I'd ever been to in my entire life. In addition to antique powder horns and wooden sleds, huge framed black and white photos of men standing on logs with pike poles decorated the thick paneled walls of the dining room, lobby and our individual rooms. All of the bathrooms had marble floors and the deck around the pool was tile instead of concrete. On either side of the pool were two enormous hot tubs that could easily hold a dozen people each. The dining room had linen table clothes and napkins and the chandeliers were made of real elk antlers. All of the ski run names had something to do with logging, like *Cold Deck*, *The Log Jam*, and *The Sluice*.

We had already eaten lunch at a fast-food place on the way up, so as soon as we dumped our stuff in our rooms we bought our lift tickets and rented skis. Everybody except for Greg had been skiing before, so Matthew and I helped him figure out how to put his ski boots on and we started walking outside.

"It's really hard to walk in these things," Greg said.

"Loosen your boot at the top and it'll be easier," Matthew suggested.

"Just don't forget to tighten it up again when you get your skis on," I said.

Matthew and I stepped into our skis. Matthew dropped his sunglasses onto his face and took off toward Nick and Evan who were waiting in line with their snowboards for the lift up to the *Choker*.

I looked at Greg, standing there holding his skis and his poles. I really wanted to hit the slopes, but I found myself thinking about how he'd been the only one to wait for me while I had recovered from my roller coaster incident.

"You want me to teach you?" I asked him.

"Naw," he said. "You don't have to do that. My dad should be out here pretty quick and he can show me what to do."

"Well," I said, "I'll at least help you get started while you're waiting."

By the time Mr. White found us, Greg could turn and stop pretty good. I said goodbye and headed off toward *The Choker*. When I returned to the lodge to get changed for dinner, Greg had been down *The Log Jam* three times and *Cold Deck* twice.

"Don't be surprised if you're really sore tomorrow," I told Greg. We were sitting in the hot tub. Nick and Evan and Matthew had just left to join the girls who were swimming in the pool.

"Great," he said, sinking deeper into the water.

I started fiddling with the knobs on the side of the hot tub.

"I think you're supposed to be able to adjust the pressure of these jets," I said, twisting one of them until it came off in my hand. "*Oops.*"

"I saw this thing on TV one time where someone was trying to drown somebody in a Jacuzzi," Greg said.

"Should I be scared?" I asked, trying to screw the nozzle back on. He laughed.

"Maybe. Anyway, she survived because she breathed in air from the jets while her head was underwater, but she pretended to be dead."

I furrowed my brow at him. "I don't think you could really do that . . . *could you?*"

A few minutes later when Laci got in the hot tub with us we were both coughing and sputtering.

"What in the *world* are you two doing?" she asked.

"Trying to see if you can survive by breathing in air from the jets underwater," I explained.

"You can't," Greg added as she sat down.

"Here." I handed her the nozzle and pointed to where it had come from. "Why don't you see if you can get this thing back on . . . it fell off."

She twisted it right back into place.

"That figures," I muttered.

"What does?" she asked.

"Oh, just the way you act, that's all."

"What are you talking about?" she said.

"You just always act like you're so *perfect* all the time."

"I do not!" she said. "What's your problem? You asked me to put it back on and I did!"

"Whatever," I mumbled, laying my head back and closing my eyes. I opened them again just in time to see Greg holding one hand up with his fingers in a circle for Laci to see. I had noticed him giving Laci this signal before, just like I'd seen him putting his forefinger and thumb together as if he were pinching a grain of salt and holding it up for Tanner to see. Tanner would always shake his head and laugh, but when I asked Tanner what it meant, he wouldn't tell me.

"What's that mean?" I asked them.

"Nothing!" Laci said quickly.

"Oh, come on! I won't tell anyone. Tell me what it means."

"NO!" Laci said, glancing at Greg.

"Sorry," Greg shook his head at me.

"Well, what about this?" I pinched my forefinger and thumb together.

"Nope. All my hand signals are secret! You wouldn't want me to share your secrets . . . *would* you?"

"You mean '*chop, chop*'? Sure . . . knock yourself out. I'm not the one who's turning into a long-haired, hippie-freak."

Laci laughed.

"No," he said, smiling. "I mean *any* kind of secrets," and I knew he was talking about Samantha so I shut up quick.

The rest of the kids climbed out of the pool and walked over to the hot tub.

"Hey!" Natalie grinned. "Let's join the Polar Bear Club!"

Laci furrowed her brow at her. "The *what?*"

"You know," Evan said. "The Polar Bear Club!"

"What's that?" I asked.

"You mean when people go jumping into an icy lake in the middle of winter?" Greg asked and they nodded their heads.

"Oh yeah!" Laci replied. "I've seen that on TV!"

"I've seen it too," I said, "but it's usually a bunch of old men in swim caps."

"Let's do it!" Greg said. "It'll be fun!"

"Get back to me when I'm an old man," I told them, but Laci and Greg were already climbing out of the hot tub and I felt another roller coaster ride coming on.

We snuck down to the little pond that the ski resort used for making artificial snow. We were already hopping up and down in bare feet, rubbing our arms.

"This is *stupid*," I said.

"On the count of three," Nick said, ignoring me. "One . . . Two . . . Three!" they yelled as we all dashed forward.

I was the only one who didn't stop.

It was a good thing that nobody else jumped in because the breath was absolutely *sucked* from my lungs and I couldn't move. They all had to pull me out and practically carry me back to the swim complex, apologizing the whole time, promising me they'd meant to jump too and saying that they were really, *really* sorry. I couldn't say anything back – my teeth were clattering so hard that I honestly thought I was going to crack a tooth. They probably thought I was being grumpy again, but if my mouth had been working properly they would have actually seen a smile.

I was the only person I knew who was in the Polar Bear Club.

Bolstered by my bravery (or stupidity) the night before, I screwed up the courage to try *The Sluice* the next day. It was the hardest run at the resort and I was quite proud of myself by the time I made it to the bottom without falling.

"I could do it too if I made turns that wide," Greg said. He'd been watching me.

"Yeah, right!"

"I could," he insisted. "I just don't want to right now."

"I'll bet you wouldn't even get on the lift!"

"Oh, I would too," he said.

"I'll bet you ten dollars you won't try it!"

"Are you serious?"

"Yup," I nodded. "Ten bucks."

He bit his lip and looked up at the top.

"I just have to *try* it?" he asked. "I don't have to actually succeed?"

"It'll be worth ten bucks to watch you take off your skis at the top and scoot all the way down on your butt!"

He stuck his gloved hand out.

"Deal," he said, and we shook.

I think the ride up took a lot longer than he expected because he seemed pretty nervous by the time we got off the lift. I was actually feeling a bit sorry for him as he pushed himself back and forth at the top of the hill – "warming up" is what he said. He finally adjusted his goggles and pushed himself forward, shooting straight down the hill. I knew right away that he was going *way* too fast.

"Turn!" I yelled. "TURN!"

He turned. He headed straight toward the edge of the narrow run. After that he shot through a stand of trees and soared off the edge of a rocky crag, disappearing from sight.

Oh crap. I jammed my pole into the ski release, having to try about five times before I finally hit it right and popped my ski off. Then I stepped on the release of the other one and scrambled down the slope, falling and sliding toward where I had seen him go off. The entire way down I kept wondering how I could best alert the ski patrol, what I was going to tell his dad, and *why* I had goaded him into doing this.

I spotted his red parka first. He was lying on his back, about twenty yards into the woods. His skis were gone, but his poles were still strapped to his wrists.

He wasn't moving.

"Greg!" I shouted, "are you okay?"

No response.

Oh crap.

"Greg!" I was close enough now to tell that his eyes were closed.

"Oh, man . . . Greg! *Greg!*" I wanted to jostle him to wake him up but I was thinking about neck injuries and I knew I shouldn't move him.

"I gotta go get help . . ." I said under my breath, not wanting to leave him alone. I started to turn away and I thought I heard him groan.

"Greg?"

"David . . ." he said, so softly that I could barely hear him.

He was alive! Thank God he was alive!

"Greg!" I shouted. He still hadn't opened his eyes. "You're going to be okay! I'm going to go get help."

"David . . ." he whispered again.

"What?"

He opened his eyes, propped himself up on his elbows, and smiled at me broadly.

"YOU owe ME ten bucks!"

I paid Greg his ten dollars at lunch and he held up ten fingers to me every time he caught my eye for the rest of the trip.

"What's that mean?" Laci asked us when she saw him do it at dinner.

"Nothing," I said. "All his hand signals are *secret*, remember?"

Greg smiled and shrugged and she walked off.

"Don't worry," he said in a hushed voice. "I won't tell anyone how scared you were."

"I was *not* scared," I said. "I couldn't care less what happens to you."

"Uh-huh," he smiled.

"Oh, shut-up."

We had one last evening of fun that night at the swim complex, racing against each other in the pool, making cannonballs, and building pyramids with the girls standing on our shoulders. I spent a lot of time in the hot tub and I decided that when I was out on my own I was going to have one in my house.

"This has been great!" I said as we were drying off before going back to our rooms. "I hope we get to come back here next year."

Everyone else nodded and murmured their agreement – everyone that is except for Laci. I barely noticed, but probably I should have sensed that something else would be in store for us the next year.

~ ~ ~

IT WAS THE end of February and we had each just finished saying grace. Mom jumped up and ran into the kitchen because she had forgotten to put butter on the table.

"Hey, Mom?"

"What?"

"Can you watch Charlotte next weekend?"

She came back in and put the butter down in front of Dad.

"Why?"

"So Mrs. White can go ice fishing with us. We need a chaperone for Laci."

"Just Laci?" she asked, sitting down.

"Yeah." Apparently nobody else thought ice fishing was going to be all that much fun. Only Greg and Laci and I had signed up to go. Mr. White had already put down a deposit for two places at Cross Lake, but if we didn't find a female chaperone he was going to cancel the whole trip.

"I'd love to help," she said, "but I can't. Friday's a teacher workday remember?"

"Mr. White's taking the day off . . ." (Mr. White taught chemistry and physics at the high school . . . my mom taught math.)

"*Mr. White* asked for the day off a long time ago," she said, "and *Mr. White* is not leading a teacher workshop at the elementary school."

"Couldn't you take her to work with you?" I asked. I really wanted to go ice fishing.

"That won't work," she said, shaking her head.

"Why not?"

"I just told you. I'm *leading* a workshop on Friday and I won't be able to do that if I'm chasing Charlotte around all day."

"*Please* . . ." I begged.

31

"No," she said. "I'm really sorry David, but it just *won't work.*"

I sighed. I was *never* going to get to go ice fishing.

"I could watch her on Friday while you're at work," Jessica suggested.

I loved Jessica.

"Now *that*," Mom said, "might work."

"Why are you laughing at me?" Laci wanted to know.

We had just met at the church parking lot and Greg and I were wearing our winter jackets, but they were unzipped. We had on sneakers, no gloves, and no hat. Laci showed up in her ski parka, ski pants, winter boots, ear muffs, insulated gloves and a scarf.

"We aren't going to the Arctic!" I said.

"But we're going *ice* fishing!"

"Yeah," I agreed, "but we're going to be fishing *on* the ice, not *in* it!"

She looked at me, uncertainly.

"Laci," I explained, "Cross Lake is about an hour from here. It's going to be the same temperature there that it is here."

"Oh," she said, looking a little disappointed as she unwound her scarf.

I'd been to Cross Lake plenty in the summer, but it looked a lot different in the winter. When I'd been up there with my dad or Tanner's dad, the marina had always been full of people playing video games and pool and ordering fried onion rings or snow cones. Now it was all but empty and a sign said it was only open Friday thru Sunday. The big field to the right of the marina had always been filled with little vacant shanties during the summer. Now the field was empty and the shanties were spread out all across the frozen lake.

The little shanties, it turns out, were called fish houses. Each one had four cots, a cook stove, a lantern, and two holes drilled for ice fishing. Outside each fish house were two more holes.

We went to the marina to pay the balance on the fish houses and to rent fishing equipment. The fishing poles were only about two feet long. Mr. White said that they didn't need to be as long as regular poles because there was no casting involved with ice fishing. All you did was drop your baited hook down into the water and wait for the bobber to move.

We sat around all Friday afternoon waiting for our bobbers to move.

"Are you sure you know what you're doing?" Greg asked his dad after a couple of hours.

"Yes," he said. "Sometimes they just aren't biting."

"Have you been ice fishing before?" Laci asked him.

"Oh, sure," he nodded. "I went to college at State. We used to go to Makasoi Lake and ice fish in the winter all the time."

"Hey!" I told him. "My parents went to State!"

"I know," he said.

"Did you guys know each other?"

"No," he said, shaking his head. "Your parents graduated before Greg's mom and I got there."

"Oh," I said. "That's where Jessica's applying to go. I'm probably going to go there too."

"It's a great school," he replied. "What do you want to major in?"

"I don't have any idea."

"Well, that's okay," he said. "You've got plenty of time. Do you know where you want to go, Laci?"

"Probably Collens College."

"My mother went there," he told her.

"Really?" she asked, and he nodded.

"Where's *that?*" I asked, making a face.

"About another hour north of here," she said.

"I've never even heard of it."

"It's a small, women's college," she explained.

"They only let small women go there?" I asked.

"Very funny," she said, but Greg and Mr. White laughed.

"Where do you want to go, Greg?" Laci asked.

"State," he replied without hesitation. "I'm going to be an engineer and they've got one of the best engineering programs in the country."

"You want to drive a train?" I asked.

"No," Greg said, seriously. "Not *that* kind of engineer . . ."

"I *know* what kind of engineer you meant," I said. "I'm not stupid."

"Are you sure?" Laci asked, and I smirked at her.

"Well," Mr. White said, standing up. "I'm going to walk around and talk to some of the other fishermen—"

Laci cleared her throat.

"Pardon me," he told her. "Fisher*people*. I'll be back in a little while."

"Sorry we aren't catching anything," Greg said after he was gone.

"Oh," I said, waving my hand at him dismissively. "Don't worry about it. Fishing's not about the fish."

"It's not?" Laci said.

"No!" I said. "Tanner and Mike and I came up here camping with my dad one time and all we caught were a few sunfish, but it was one of the best weekends of my life."

She raised an eyebrow at me.

"Oh you wouldn't understand," I said.

"Mike will get to come here with us next year," Greg said.

"Maybe," Laci said.

"Yeah," I agreed. "Sometimes he has to miss a lot of stuff because of his dad."

"I've never met his dad," Greg said.

"He's sick a lot."

"Is that whose name I see on the prayer list at church all the time?" Greg asked, and Laci and I both nodded.

"What's wrong with him?" Greg asked.

Laci and I looked at each other and hesitated.

"I'm not sure exactly," I finally said. "Something with his kidneys maybe?"

"Or liver? Something like that," Laci nodded. "All I know is that he's been sick ever since I've known Mike."

"Yeah," I agreed. "It seems like he's always going into the hospital, or just getting home from the hospital. You never see him outside or anything."

"The only time I think I've ever seen him outside was at that birthday party Mike had with the clown when we were little," Laci said, looking at me. "Remember?"

I nodded.

"He didn't even stay for all of it," I added. "He went back inside before it was over."

"Can't they do something for him?" Greg asked.

"I guess not," I said. "Mike doesn't seem to want to talk about it a lot . . ."

"So," Laci finished, "we don't ask."

After Mr. White got back and informed us that *no one* was catching *anything*, Mrs. White called us in for dinner. I was really glad she'd been able to come along . . . we had lasagna.

After dinner we dragged our sleeping bags out onto the ice because the stars were so brilliant.

"There's the Big Dipper," Laci said, pointing.

"That's the only constellation I know," I said.

"It's actually not a constellation," Mr. White told me. "It's an asterism."

"A what?"

"An asterism. An asterism is a small group of stars that you can pick out easily . . . like the Big Dipper. It's part of the constellation, Ursa Major."

He tried to show us Ursa Major.

"Do you see it?" he asked.

"I'm not sure," Laci said. "Maybe."

"It's a lot easier to see asterisms," Mr. White explained. "They can help you locate the different constellations."

He spent over an hour with us showing us different asterisms and constellations and explaining how things would look different in the summer sky.

Greg's mom finally stood up, said goodnight, and dragged her sleeping bag into the fish house she was sharing with Laci.

"Can we sleep out here tonight, Dad?" Greg asked.

"I guess if you want to . . ." he said. "I'm cold and tired though. I'm going back in where it's warm."

I was getting cold too, but I wasn't about to admit it. Laci started doling out extra clothing from her duffle bag to Greg.

"Do you want to use my dad's electric hunting socks?" she asked me.

"Laci," I said. "I'm a member of the Polar Bear Club. Members of the Polar Bear Club do *not* wear electric socks."

"Suit yourself," she replied, snuggling into her mummy bag.

A few minutes later my teeth started chattering – nowhere near as hard as they had at the ski lodge, but hard enough that Laci and Greg could hear them and I couldn't stop them.

"Propane hand warmer?" she asked, holding it up in front of me.

"Oh, shut up," I said, snatching it from her.

"Look!" Laci cried. "A shooting star!"

"Actually," Greg told her, "it's a meteor–"

"Oh, shut up," I said again.

We lay there quietly for a few moments.

"You know," I said, clutching the hand warmer to my chest, "I don't believe in wishes . . . but, if you *were* going to make one . . . what would you wish for?"

"That's easy!" Laci answered. "I'd wish for–"

"And," I interrupted, "you can't wish for world peace or anything like that. It's got to be something selfish."

"Oh," she said. "Well, I'm going to have to think about that then. One of you guys go first."

"Greg?"

"Well, I'm going to have to take a lot of hard math classes and stuff, so . . . I'll wish for really good grades . . ."

"*Wow!*" I said. "World peace and good grades. And you two say that *I'm* no fun."

"We don't say that you're no fun," Greg corrected. "We say that you're grumpy."

"Can't you think up something a little more interesting than good grades?" I asked. "Something materialistic . . . you know? Just for fun . . . sky's the limit!"

"Okay," Greg said. "I guess a Corvette."

"Sky's the limit, remember? How about a Ferrari?"

"Can it be red?"

"Sure."

"Okay then," he said. "A red Ferrari. Convertible though. I want my hair to be able to flow in the breeze . . ."

"Oh, brother. Okay . . . a red Ferrari. Laci? Did you think up something yet?"

"Yeah!" She said. "I'd have my own amusement park! I had *so* much fun at Six Flags!"

"Uhhhggg," I moaned. "That was *not* fun."

"What was wrong with Six Flags?"

"Don't ask," Greg replied. "What about you, Dave?"

"My own ski resort," I said. "Now *that* was fun!" I didn't tell them that my wish also included having the whole place to myself – just me and Samantha.

"You know," Laci said, "about the ski trip. I've been thinking–"

"Oh, no . . ." I said.

"What?" she asked.

"Nothing."

"*Oh, no*, what?" she demanded.

"Every time you say 'I've been thinking,' we wind up in a mess!"

"That is *not* true!" she said.

"What about last summer?" I asked her. She didn't answer.

"What happened last summer?" Greg wanted to know.

"Nothing!" Laci snapped.

"Oh," Greg said. "This sounds good. What happened?"

"Laci got this bright idea–" I started, but she cut me off.

"Shut up, David or I'll take my hand warmer back."

"Come get it!" I dared her.

"This sounds *really* good," Greg said. "Come on, tell me."

"Oh, don't worry," I assured him, "I'm gonna tell you."

Laci flopped over onto her stomach and buried her head into her pillow while I told him.

Laci had decided that our Sunday school needed to help out by visiting people at the local nursing home. She had also heard that there are people who bring trained therapy animals into nursing homes for the elderly to pet. According to Laci, elderly people who are able to pet animals on a regular basis live longer and are healthier and happier than those who don't.

"Now, about this same time," I told Greg, "Laci learned about a volunteer program at the animal shelter for dog walkers . . ."

"Oh, no . . ." Greg said. "Don't tell me your Sunday school teacher went along with this?"

"Yup!" I said. "It was Ms. Tanya . . . you may have noticed that she's not a Sunday school teacher anymore . . ."

"STOP IT!" Laci yelled into her pillow.

"So, anyway," I continued, "we show up at the nursing home, and each of us has at least one dog on a leash . . ."

"Did the nursing home know you were coming?" Greg asked.

"Well, they knew *we* were coming, but I don't think they knew about the dogs . . ."

"Yes they did!" Laci yelled into her pillow. "Yes they did! We told them we were bringing therapy dogs!"

"Oh! But, we *weren't* bringing therapy dogs, were we Laci? We were bringing dogs that had been trapped in a five by ten cage for two weeks and probably hadn't had twenty combined minutes of obedience school, *weren't* we, Laci?"

I couldn't tell if Laci was laughing or crying, but I plowed ahead.

"So anyway, the first thing that happens is that this huge Great Dane—"

"It was *not* a Great Dane," Laci said, and I decided she was laughing.

"Okay, this HUGE mutt, plops its paws up on one of those medicine carts and scarfs down about thirty little paper cups full of pills. Then this nurse comes running over to us and two of the little dogs get their leashes around her ankles and she grabs at the cart to keep herself from falling and the whole thing turns over."

Greg started laughing.

"Then there's this old man sitting in a chair, and he starts poking at my dog with his cane and my dog grabs at it with his teeth and starts growling and pulling it . . ."

Greg was laughing hard now.

"And then Ashlyn's dog slipped his collar off and took off down the hall and disappeared."

"Did you ever find it?" Greg managed to ask.

"Yes, of course we found it," Laci said. "Do you think we just left it there?"

"Yeah," I agreed. "We found it all right. All we had to do was follow the shrieks of this old lady who was lying on her bed and trying to shoo him away with her remote control."

"Happy?" Laci asked me after Greg and I had quit laughing quite so hard.

"Yeah . . ." I said. "Pretty happy. Thanks for asking."

"Do you think you can stop laughing long enough to listen to what I was going to say now?" she asked.

"Maybe."

"Okay," she said. "I don't think we should go on a ski trip next year."

"What!?" I practically yelled. I definitely wasn't laughing now. "Why in the *world* would you not want to go back there!? That was fun! You had fun too!"

"I did have fun," she admitted. "A *lot* of fun. But, it's not always about having fun . . ."

I sighed. I could almost tell where this was going.

"We spent a bunch of money going skiing," she said. "I was thinking that we could earn the same amount of money next year and do something more important."

"Whatcha got in mind?" Greg asked.

"I think we should go on a mission trip to Mexico," she said.

"Do they eat dog there?" I asked. "Because we could stop by the animal shelter first . . ."

"No," Greg said. "I think that's Vietnam . . ."

"Come on, you guys . . . I'm serious," Laci said. "We could do something really good . . . you know? Something that could have . . . *eternal* value."

40

I sighed again. I already knew our ski trip for next year was off.

"What do you think?" she asked Greg. I don't think she wanted to know what I thought.

"¡Vámonos!" Greg said.

"What's that mean?" I asked.

"It's Spanish for 'let's go'!"

"You speak Spanish?" Laci asked him.

"No," he explained. "Charlotte watches *Dora the Explorer* all the time."

When I woke up in the morning I was in our fish house. I vaguely remembered moving inside after even Laci's electric socks had failed to warm me up. Greg was inside too, still sleeping. His dad was warming a pot of water on the stove.

"Instant coffee," he asked, "or hot chocolate?"

No one had ever offered me coffee before . . . instant or otherwise.

"Um . . . coffee."

He handed me a mug. It smelled really good. I took a sip.

"Uhg!" I said, trying not to spit it out.

"Cream and sugar?" he asked, smiling.

"Yes, please," I said. I added about five tablespoons of sugar and some cream and stirred it with a spoon. I took another sip.

"Better?" Mr. White asked.

"Not really."

"Want some hot chocolate?" he offered again.

"Yes, please."

Greg stirred and stretched and sat up. His dad handed him some hot chocolate.

"You don't like coffee either?" I asked.

"I don't know," Greg said, rubbing his eyes. "My parents never let me try it."

Mr. White winked at me and I smiled.

"What time did you boys come in?" he asked.

"I don't know," Greg said. "I really don't even remember coming in at all . . . Dave?"

"I don't know," I said. "I don't remember coming in either."

We looked at each other.

"You don't suppose we left Laci out there all by herself – *do you?*" Greg said.

"Naw . . ." I answered, shaking my head.

"Are you sure?"

"Not really . . ."

We both jumped up and looked out the door. We didn't see anything but ice.

"She must have gone in too," I said.

"Either that or a bear dragged her off . . ."

"There aren't any bears around here!" I said.

"Are you sure?"

"Pretty sure . . ."

"Why don't you two act like gentlemen and go next door and make sure she got in safely?" Mr. White asked. We pulled on our jackets and walked to the other fish house. Greg knocked on the door.

"Come in . . ." Mrs. White called. Greg opened the door and we both peeked in, relieved to see Laci standing next to the stove, stirring something in a pot.

"Good morning," Mrs. White said.

"Good morning," we both answered. Then we sang in unison, "Good morning, Laci."

She looked at us suspiciously.

"What's up with you two?" she asked.

"Nothing," I said, smiling.

42

"Just glad to see you," Greg said. "That's all."

"Let me guess," she said. "You're over here to mooch breakfast."

"That would be good," I nodded. "All we have next door is hot chocolate and coffee."

"There's coffee?" Mrs. White asked.

"It's instant," I warned her.

"Better than nothing," she said. "I'll be back in a minute."

She left and Laci spooned some oatmeal into bowls for all three of us.

"Hey Laci," Greg said when we were finished. "Do you have some barrettes or something? My hair is really starting to get in my eyes."

"Oh, brother," I muttered.

She started digging around in a small duffle.

"Laci!" I said. "DO NOT give him barrettes! He CAN'T wear barrettes!"

"Relax," Laci told me, pulling out a brush.

"Come here," she told Greg. He scooted around until he was sitting in front of her with his back to her. She started brushing his hair.

"A guy who is comfortable with his masculinity can wear barrettes if he wants to," Greg grinned at me.

"*I'm* not comfortable with your masculinity," I replied.

"Oh, really?" he asked.

"Yeah, really."

"Well let me ask you something then," he said. "Which one of us is sitting here with a pretty girl running her hands through his hair?"

Laci giggled.

I hated it when I had to admit that he was right. I wondered briefly if Sam would want to run her fingers through my hair if I started letting it grow out.

43

"Here," Laci told Greg. "Turn this way."

She worked on his hair some more and finally patted him on the knee.

"I'm afraid I'm going to have to agree with Dave on this one," she said. "No barrettes. Even *I* think that would be a little too much." She held a mirror up for him to look into. "Just tuck it behind your ears like this until it's long enough for a ponytail."

"How much longer is that going to take?" he asked her, turning his head and looking into the mirror.

"Probably by summer . . ."

"Oh, brother," I said.

We took our poles back to the marina and rented ones called "tip-ups" instead. These consisted of two poles . . . one that lay across the hole and one that pointed down into the hole. When (and if) a fish were to bite, a bright red flag would pop up. You didn't have to pay quite as much attention to the tip-ups as you did a regular pole with a bobber – that had gotten old pretty fast.

Even though we could get a lot further away from our poles and be able to tell if we had a bite, by lunchtime we were sick of doing that too. Mr. White said he would keep an eye on things and promised to let us know if a flag popped up. We headed off to the marina.

There were video games and a pool table inside the marina. I pushed quarters into the pool table before Laci could even protest.

"They rent ice skates here," she said. "Let's go ice skating!"

"No," I said. "Ice skating is for girls."

"No, it's not," she said. "Come on, I don't want to skate alone."

"I want to play pool," I told her. I hadn't gotten to play since the swim complex had closed down at the end of the summer.

"Please," she begged.

44

"Sorry." I wasn't going to tell her that I'd never ice skated before and I wasn't about to try it now. "I've got to beat Greg at pool."

She bit her lip. "What if *I* beat *you* at pool?"

"Yeah, right," I scoffed.

"I'm serious," she said. "What if I beat you at pool? Will you skate then?"

"What do I get if *I* win?" I asked.

She thought for a moment.

"I'll join the Polar Bear Club," she finally decided.

"How're you going to do that?" I asked. "Everything's frozen solid."

"Well, then," she said. "You can fill up buckets of water and I'll lay down on the ice and you can dump freezing cold water on me."

"How many buckets?"

She bit her lip and thought for another second.

"Three."

"You've got a deal."

Laci chalked up and Greg leaned against the wall and watched, an amused smile on his face.

"Ladies first," I said.

"Oh, no," she said, shaking her head. "I'm not having you backing out because I got to break or something. You go first."

"Fine."

I broke and got nothing. Laci took her turn and got a solid in.

It was closer than I thought it would be and a *lot* closer than I wanted it to be. Laci had one ball left and mine were all gone. It was my turn and Laci's ball was blocking the eight ball.

"Pool is all about physics," Greg said as I was lining up my shot. He'd been pretty quiet until then and I looked up at him and sighed heavily.

"I'm just saying," he said, holding up his hands, "that any shot can be made if you just use physics."

"Would you be quiet please?" I said.

45

"You don't want some advice?"

I glared at him. "No. I don't want any advice."

I got ready to shoot and he interrupted again.

"Because," he told me, "I've got some really great advice."

I put my pool stick down on the table.

"Say it," I said. "Say whatever it is you have to say and get it over with."

"Aim right here," he suggested, pointing to the edge of the table. "It'll hit the eight ball in and deflect hers out of the way."

I didn't know that much about physics, but it seemed to make sense.

"Okay," I said. "Will you move now?"

He nodded.

"And be quiet?"

He nodded again, smiled, and stepped back against the wall.

I took aim and hit the cue ball. It knocked Laci's ball out of the way, but missed the eight ball and shot into the pocket. They both burst out laughing.

"I could have told you that wasn't going to work!" Laci said.

I laid my head down on the pool table.

"Why didn't you?" I yelled.

"Because," she said, still laughing. "I really want to go ice skating."

Fortunately ice skating wasn't a lot different from roller blading so I caught on pretty quick and didn't embarrass myself too badly. Apparently they roller blade in Florida *a lot* because Greg was literally skating circles around me and Laci all afternoon.

At one point he sped off to check on our red flags back at the fish houses and Laci and I were left alone by the marina.

"Hey, Laci," I said, trying to figure out how to go backwards.

"What?"

"You wanna help me get even with Greg?"

"For what?" she asked.

"Well, for his little physics lesson in there for one thing," I said. He'd already invented a hand signal for it, dragging a claw through the air like fingernails on a blackboard. *Scratch.*

"Why would I want to help you do that?" she asked. "That worked out pretty well for me."

"Well, that's not the only reason," I said. "I've been wanting to get even with him for something else too."

"What?" she asked.

I told her about how he had pretended to be hurt after he'd soared off *The Sluice* when we were skiing.

"I don't know . . ." she hesitated.

"Come on," I coaxed her. "It'll be fun . . . nothing *too* bad."

"Tell me what you've got in mind."

Greg came back and reported that no red flags had popped up yet.

"Where's Laci?" he asked.

"She went into the marina to get some hot cocoa."

"Oh."

We skated around for a couple of minutes until she emerged, carrying a little cardboard tray with Styrofoam cups for each of us.

"Thanks," Greg and I both said.

"Oooh, that guy's mad," Laci said.

"What guy?" Greg asked.

"The guy that's working in there," Laci said, pointing toward the marina.

"Why?" I asked.

"His phone's missing."

"Did he lose it?" Greg asked.

"No," Laci said. "He accidentally left it here last night and he thinks a chuffer got it."

I decided right then that Laci was too good of a liar to ever trust again.

"What's a chuffer?" Greg wanted to know.

"You don't know what a chuffer is?" Laci asked.

Greg shook his head.

"Oh brother," I said. "Now I know why they call you guys Floridiots. Are you serious? You really don't know what a chuffer is?"

"Uh-uh."

"They probably don't have them in Florida," Laci told me.

"I guess not," I agreed.

"What's a chuffer?" Greg asked again.

"Well," Laci said, "it's kind of like a big squirrel . . ."

"Or a small raccoon," I said.

"Yeah," Laci nodded. "I think they wash their food off like raccoons do . . ."

"How did a chuffer get his phone?" Greg asked.

"Oh!" I said. "They're like little thieves with fur. They can get through cracks about this big," I held my hands about three inches apart, "and then they steal shiny stuff and hoard it away in their chuffer holes."

"My dad always calls them chuffer *troves*," Laci said. "He found one when he was hunting in Canada one year and it had a brass compass in it."

Man she lied good.

"Really?" Greg asked.

"Oh yeah," I said, nodding.

"What do they look like?" he wanted to know.

"The holes?" I asked.

"Yeah."

48

"They just look like holes in the snow," Laci said.

"Or the mud," I said. "Tanner and I found one in the summer once."

"What was in it?" Greg asked.

"I don't know," I shrugged, "nothing too great. A button, I think maybe fifty cents, a busted lure . . ."

I was doing a pretty good job too . . . I bet Laci was never going to trust me either.

"How hard are they to find?"

"Oh," Laci said, "they're real easy to find, but you only want to look for them at night."

"Why?"

"Because you don't want to go sticking your hands down in a chuffer hole during the day," I said. "They bite!"

"They only bite during the day?"

"No," Laci said. "They only stay in their holes during the day. At night they go out looking for food and more shiny stuff."

"Yeah," I said. "I've only looked for them at night before."

"Can we look tonight?" Greg asked.

Bingo.

"Well," I shrugged, "I guess we could."

"I doubt we'll find anything good," Laci said.

"It wouldn't hurt to try," Greg said.

"No," I agreed. "It wouldn't hurt to try. You never know what you might find."

Laci managed to give me the thumbs up at dinner. Our hand signal may not have been as imaginative as Greg's, but it got the point across: I knew that her "trip to the bathhouse" before dinner had been successful.

After dinner we headed back to the marina to play some more video games. I'd convinced Greg it was best not to mention what we were going to do to his mom and dad.

"Parent's always get all worried about rabies and stuff," I'd said. "Better to beg forgiveness later than ask permission first. We'll just play some video games, and on the way back we'll look around for a few chuffer holes . . . no big deal."

After we'd played video games for about an hour, Laci said all the chuffers were probably out for the night and that we ought to get going.

I let Laci take the lead since she'd planted everything.

"Here's one!" she cried, shining her light on a hole.

She tugged off her glove and put her hand down into the hole. She pulled out a barrette and a dime.

"No phone," she said.

"Don't give Greg that barrette," I warned her.

"Don't worry," she said, putting it in her pocket.

I got to check the next hole we found. I took off my glove and pulled out a pair of tweezers and a quarter.

"Are you sure that's all that's in there?" Laci asked.

I reached in again and found her nail file.

"You can look in the next one, Greg," I told him.

"Okay," he said. "This is cool."

"They don't have thieving alligators or anything in Florida?"

"Alligators, yes . . . thieving ones, no."

At the next hole Greg knelt down and started to reach in.

"You've got to take your glove off first," I said.

"Why?"

"Because if it's something small like money you won't be able to feel it and you'll just shove it under the snow and you'll never find it."

"Oh." He pulled off a glove and tentatively stuck his hand in the hole.

50

"Ugh!" he said, pulling something out.

"What is it?"

"I don't know," he said, holding his light on it. "I think it's a fish."

It was. A minnow.

"Oh, yeah," I nodded. "Sometimes they hoard fish too."

"Keep looking," Laci urged. "There's probably something under the fish."

He stuck his hand back in and pulled out more fish, and more, and more.

"There's nothing else in here," he said.

"Are you sure?" Laci asked.

"I can't find anything," he said.

"Did you put anything else in there Laci?" I asked her.

"No," she answered. "Pretty much just fish in that one."

"Do you want your nail file back?"

"Yes, please," she nodded, "and my tweezers too."

"Oh!" Greg cried, "I'm going to kill both of you!"

But Laci had already started running, so he just tried to kill me.

We dropped Laci off at her fish house and then went to ours. Mr. White was reading by the lantern light when we came in.

"Have fun?" he asked.

"Yep!" I said.

After a moment he glanced up at us.

"What's that smell?"

"Fish," I said.

"What's all over your jackets?"

"Minnow parts . . ." Greg said.

"*Minnow parts?*"

"We kind of had a fish fight," I said.

"A fish fight?"

"Yeah," Greg said. "After Laci and David took me chuffer hunting."

"We weren't hunting for chuffers," I corrected him. "We were hunting for chuffer *holes* . . ."

"Chuffer holes?" Mr. White asked. "Is there any chance that's a lot like snipe hunting?"

I nodded and grinned.

"So is Laci covered with minnow parts too?" he asked.

"No," I said. "She pretty much just stood there and laughed at us."

"I see," Mr. White said.

"As a matter of fact," Greg said, "Laci did a lot of standing around laughing at us today . . ."

"Oh, really?" Mr. White asked.

"Yeah," I said, furrowing my brow. "She did."

We decided that Laci was probably going to be pretty suspicious of anything we tried to pull at this point and on such short notice we couldn't come up with anything too creative anyway. The best we could do was to listen for the door of the ladies' fish hut to slam shut when they left for the bathhouse to brush their teeth and wash up before going to bed. We convinced Mr. White to stick his head out the door.

"Dana?" he called. "Oh, you go on ahead, Laci . . . I need to talk to Mrs. White for a second."

He held the door open for Mrs. White and she stepped into our fish house. Mr. White looked at us.

"Don't you two make me sorry that I helped you," he said, pointing a finger at us and we shook our heads at him.

"What are you three up to?" Mrs. White asked.

"Nothing . . ." we all said in unison and she rolled her eyes at us.

Greg and I snuck outside and could see Laci off in the distance, nearing the bathhouse. As soon as we started after her I slipped on the ice.

"Ooof!"

"Be quiet!" Greg whispered.

"I'm *sorry!*" I whispered back. "I'll try to break my neck more *quietly* next time."

"Get up here." Greg stuck out his hand and helped me up.

We saw the bathhouse lights come on. That was good . . . she was alone. We crept up to the door and quietly sat down, our backs firm against it.

She took *forever.*

"What is she *doing* in there?" I whispered.

"Shhhhh."

"What if she decides to wait for your mom?"

That time I got a "shhhhh" and an elbow in the ribs.

"Ow."

"Would you *shut-up!?*" Greg whispered. I shut up.

Finally we heard footsteps coming toward the door and heard her flip off the light switch. We braced ourselves against the door.

Thump.

Thump, thump.

The light came back on.

Thump. Thump, thump.

There was a long pause.

"I know you guys are out there . . ."

I put my hand over my mouth to keep from laughing out loud.

"All right, that's enough," she said. "Let me out!"

Thump, thump, thump.

"LET ME OUT!"

Thump, kick, bang.

"You guys . . . come on, you guys . . ."

I heard her sigh and then it was quiet.

"What's she doing?" I whispered.

"I don't know," Greg whispered back, "but when she starts pushing again we'll move on the count of three and she'll come flying out."

But Laci didn't push again. Instead, Laci took her shampoo bottle quietly to the sink and filled it to the top with water. Then she shook it, snapped open the squirt top, aimed it at the crack under the door and emptied it. By the time we felt it soak through our jeans to our skin the bottle was empty.

"*What the* . . ."

Both of us reached our hands down and got our gloves covered with soapy goo.

"Oh, man!" Greg said and we both scrambled to our feet. Greg slipped in the goo and grabbed my arm, trying to save himself, but we both fell hard.

This time Laci didn't have any trouble getting the door open. She peeked down at us and smiled and when we got back to our fish house Mr. White said that we smelled like coconuts.

The next day, while Mr. and Mrs. White were finishing packing up and turning in the rented equipment, Greg and Laci and I went up by the parking lot and sat at a picnic table.

"Let's play cards," Greg said, pulling a deck out of his backpack.

"Whatdya wanna play?" I asked.

"Idiot's poker."

"I don't know how to play . . ." Laci told him.

"Me neither," I said.

"It's real easy." He dealt each one of us a card.

"Don't look at it," he said. He picked up his card and held it up to his forehead so that Laci and I could see what it was (an eight of hearts), but he couldn't.

"Okay," he said. "Now you hold your cards up and don't look at 'em."

I slapped my card onto my forehead and Laci did the same. She had a queen of spades.

"Now what?" Laci said.

"Now you have to decide if you think you can beat the other two."

"But . . ." I said, "I don't know what I have."

"Exactly."

Could I beat a queen of spades? I was trying to figure out statistically what my chances were of beating Laci's card when she said, "I'm out."

"Why'd ya do that?" I asked. "You had a good card!"

"I did?" She looked at it. "Oh . . ."

"No talking!" Greg said. "You can't go out Laci. You have to bet."

"With what?"

He pulled a bag of marshmallows out of his backpack and gave us each seven.

"Now we have to start over . . ."

We laid our cards down – I'd had a jack of clubs.

"Okay," he said. "Let's try this again. Hold your card up, NO TALKING, and just put your marshmallows in front of you to bet."

He dealt again. Laci held up a four of clubs and Greg a six of spades. I could beat that easy. I put all seven marshmallows in front of me. So did Laci and so did Greg.

We all showed our cards. I had a two of diamonds. Greg took all of our marshmallows.

Laci and I looked quizzically at each other and Greg handed out more marshmallows and cards.

Laci held up an ace of diamonds, and Greg a queen of clubs. None of us put any marshmallows out. We looked at our cards. I'd had a king. We all started laughing.

"What's this called again?" Laci asked as Greg dealt out three more cards.

"Idiot's poker."

I held my card up to my forehead. Laci and Greg were doing the same thing when Mr. and Mrs. White walked up to us. We must have looked so stupid. All three of us burst out laughing.

"I brought the camera," Mrs. White said, "and I forgot to take pictures all weekend. Let me at least get one now before we leave."

She walked to the edge of the table and we put our cards down and faced her, smiling.

"Everybody say 'cheese'," she said.

"Cheeeese!"

"Hi, honey," Mom said when I came through the front door. "Did you catch any fish?"

"No," I said, dragging my suitcase behind me through the living room.

"Oh," she said as I started up the stairs. "I'm sorry you didn't have a good time."

I honestly had no idea what she was talking about.

BY SUMMER, GREG'S hair was indeed long enough for a small ponytail. I couldn't believe it, but a few guys in our class had started growing theirs out too.

"You have groupies," I told Greg. "Are they going to donate their hair to Locks of Love too?"

"I don't know," Greg shrugged. "If they are, they didn't get the idea from me. I haven't told anybody what I'm doing except you and Laci."

"Are you serious?"

"Well," he said, "and obviously my parents. But it's like you told Laci . . . you're not supposed to let anyone but God know what you're doing when you give . . . it's supposed to be done in secret."

"She *told* you I said that?"

"Uh-huh," he said. "She also said you made her feel really bad about looking like a boy. I don't know why you're always so mean to her."

"I'm *not* always mean to her!" I said. "We were like in the fifth grade! I can't believe she told you I said that."

"Well, you hurt her feelings," he said.

"It was THREE years ago!"

"You should tell her you're sorry."

"I'm not going to tell her I'm sorry for something I did three years ago. She can just get over it."

"You should tell her you're sorry," he said again.

We saw Laci at the swim complex a lot that summer, hanging around with Natalie and Ashlyn. In addition to swimming, there was a game room with pool tables and video games. Mr. White helped me learn the *real* physics behind playing pool, but Laci and Greg still ran a claw through the air at me from time to time . . . *scratch*.

Tanner and Mike were usually there too. One day we tried to build a pyramid, like we had at the ski lodge, with Tanner and Mike and Greg and me on the bottom and Laci and Natalie and Ashlyn standing on our shoulders. We'd barely gotten a good start though when the lifeguard blew his whistle at us and made us stop. I *really* wanted to go skiing again next winter.

That wasn't going to happen though. In the fall, Laci shared her Mexico mission trip plan with everybody else in the youth group and they all thought it was a great idea. Nick and Matthew and Evan had moved up into the high school youth program led by Mrs. Kelly, and Mike and a few other kids moved up to ours from sixth grade. Mike was excited about going to Mexico.

"This is gonna be fun," he said.

"*Skiing* was fun," I told him. "*Ice fishing* was fun."

"Would you be quiet?" Greg whispered, nodding his head toward Laci, who was sitting nearby. He didn't need to let me know she was there . . . I wouldn't have bothered saying anything if I'd thought she couldn't hear me.

Each Halloween the mall hosted a trick-or-treat event in the courtyard. Non-profit groups were allowed to set up booths for free and distribute candy that the mall provided. Each trick-or-treater had to pay ten dollars to attend and all the money went to the groups running the booths. The mall didn't make any money off of it – they were just hoping to draw in customers on what would otherwise have been a slow night.

Mr. and Mrs. White and a few kids from the youth group were running one of the booths, so Greg was in charge of taking Charlotte around.

"She's a girl magnet," he'd promised when he'd convinced me to go.

He was right. Charlotte was dressed like a fluffy white lamb and said "Baaaa," whenever she held her plastic orange pumpkin out for candy.

"She's so cute!" the girls from the high school Honor Society Club exclaimed and Greg and I grinned.

Laci and Natalie were working our youth group booth with Mr. and Mrs. White.

"You can work too, if you want," Laci offered. "All the money's going toward our Mexico trip."

"No thanks," I said through my latex werewolf mask.

"It wouldn't hurt you to help out once and a while," Natalie said.

I pulled off a hairy-fingered, clawed glove and showed her one of my blisters.

"See this?" I asked. "I got this raking leaves last weekend so I could earn money to NOT go skiing."

"I like your costume," Greg told Natalie. She was dressed like a witch. Laci was a gypsy.

"Thanks," she replied. "Um . . . what are you supposed to be?"

He was in his regular clothes holding a cereal box with a knife through it.

"I'm a serial killer," he grinned. Laci and Natalie both laughed. I rolled my eyes, but no one could tell through my mask.

We walked away from the booth.

"That was mean," he said.

"What was?"

"Laci's working really hard so we can go to Mexico . . . it means a lot to her and every chance you get you complain about not being able to go skiing. It makes her feel bad."

Unseen, I rolled my eyes again.

We came to the booth run by the junior high cheerleaders and I immediately started looking for Sam. I almost didn't recognize her.

She was dressed like Cleopatra. She had on lots of sparkly green eye shadow, black eyeliner, huge fake eyelashes, and a sequined headpiece. Her tunic was silky white with a gold belt and she had gold cuffs around each wrist and a gold snake coiled around her upper arm. She was *beautiful* and I was really glad that I had my mask on because my mouth dropped open when I saw her.

"Hi, Greg," she said, squatting down in front of Charlotte. "Is this your little sister?"

He nodded.

"She's adorable!" Sam said.

"Yeah," Greg agreed, "most of the time."

"Baaa," said Charlotte.

"Who's this?" Sam asked, pointing up at me. She had on inch-long gold fingernails.

"It's David."

"Oh," she said. "Hi, David!"

I managed to lift a hairy hand to wave at her.

She put some candy in Charlotte's bucket and tickled her tummy with a gold nail.

"You'll have to tell your mommy and daddy to call me if they ever need a babysitter," Sam told her.

"Would you like that, Charlotte?" Greg asked, looking down at his sister. "Would you like for the pretty pharaoh's daughter to come and baby-sit you sometime?"

"Baaaa," Charlotte replied.

"You were *flirting* with her!" I accused after we were out of earshot.

"No I wasn't," Greg said.

"Yes, you were!"

"Noooo," Greg said, shaking his head. "I *talked* to her – which is more than I can say for you – but trust me . . . I would *not* flirt with her."

"Why not?" I asked. "What's wrong with her?"

"You know what, Charlotte?" he asked, looking down at her. "I think Davey's hopeless."

"Baaaaa."

Greg and I were in Algebra One together and so was Sam. If Sam hadn't of been in there I probably would have tried to drop it because it was *way* more work than I was interested in. Mom checked my homework every night and made me redo anything that I'd missed.

Tanner and Mike ate lunch with us every day and even before winter had set in, Mike started complaining about how we would all be going off without him again in the fall. Tanner told us this was his last season playing fall soccer with us; he was going out for the high school football team next year.

"You guys should try out too," Tanner said to me and Greg. Mike burst out laughing. Tanner and Mike were both getting a lot bigger than either one of us.

"Well," Tanner said seriously, "they could be kickers or something. A lot of teams recruit their kickers from soccer teams."

"Gee, thanks for that vote of confidence, Tanner," Greg said, "but I think I'll just stick to soccer."

I nodded in agreement.

Meanwhile, our fundraising efforts went on throughout the school year. We sold magazine subscriptions and shoveled sidewalks and wrapped Christmas presents at the mall, but by May we had only raised about half as much money as we needed for our trip to Mexico. I would like to add here that throughout it all, I had worked *hard*. Despite the fact that I always gave Laci a bad time about not being able to go skiing, I really did want to go to Mexico. I think the only two people who earned more money than me were Greg and Laci. The church board agreed to pay the rest of what we needed and Mr. White arranged all of the details. We were going to be in Mexico for a week and were all set to fly out ten days before our freshman year of high school started.

On the first day of summer vacation I got to the pool early and swam laps. I knew from past years that it was usually so crowded after lunch that it would be impossible to do anything except splash around. After I was finished I walked toward my chair, puddles of water trickling off my feet with each step. I was sitting down, toweling off my hair, when I heard Greg's voice.

"You sure were going nowhere fast," he said.

"I'm going to make varsity my freshman year," I said, looking up at him. If he hadn't of already been talking to me I wouldn't have known who he was. Most of his hair was gone.

"Well, look at you!" I said, reaching up with my hand and rubbing the top of his head. "All your little groupies are going to be crying when they see you!"

He was grinning. "I thought it would be good to have it gone during the summer."

"Did you send it off?" I asked. He nodded.

"Are you sure it was long enough?" Laci's had always been longer.

62

He nodded again.

"You have to send at least ten inches," he said. "Mine was eleven and a half."

"No more long-haired, hippie-freak," I said, shaking my head in mock despair.

"You can still call me that if you want," he smiled, "'cause I'm going to grow it out again."

"Of course you are."

"So what's this about making varsity your freshman year?" he asked me as he sat down.

I nodded. "I'm going to work out all summer and make the swim team next winter."

"What about basketball?"

"Nope," I said, shaking my head. "I'm going to swim."

Mike and Tanner had size going for them and Greg was a lot quicker than me on the court. I was tired of sitting on the bench watching them play.

"What about soccer?"

"I'm still doing soccer . . . still doing baseball. I'm just going to try swimming in the winter, that's all. Why don't you try out with me?"

"As if the basketball team could survive without me. Besides . . . the cheerleaders only work basketball and football games!"

"Don't remind me," I said.

"What event are you going to swim?"

"I don't know . . . probably freestyle."

"You should try butterfly," he suggested.

"Naw," I said, shaking my head. "I'm not any good at it."

"My dad could teach you," Greg offered. "He swam butterfly and individual medley in college. He says that if you learn to do it the right way you can really do good because most people don't ever learn how to do it right . . . there's less competition."

"That's probably exactly what I need," I said. "Less competition."

Three mornings later Mr. White was in the pool teaching me how to do the butterfly. The trick to it was getting the kicks timed exactly right during the stroke and after about thirty minutes I finally got it.

I popped up in front of him and grinned, knowing I'd done well.

"That's great, David! I'm proud of you. You're like the son I never had."

Greg was sitting behind him, dangling his feet in the water. "Thanks a lot, Dad."

"Oops, sorry Son. Forgot you were there."

"That really did look good, Davey," Greg said. "I bet you make varsity."

"Thanks!" I replied, feeling good enough to almost believe him. I worked all summer and, by the time we left for Mexico, Mr. White said my times were where they should be. I just needed to figure out some way to get the cheerleading squad to start working the swim meets and I was going to be all set.

~ ~ ~

WHEN THE MORNING came to leave for Mexico, Mom and Dad and Jessica all came to the airport to see me off. I had never been out of the country before and had never flown before, so I was pretty anxious. I'd hardly slept that night at all.

Laci was pretty excited too – she could barely sit still once we got on the plane. I know, because I sat in between her and Greg and she kept tucking her legs up underneath her and then putting them back down, shifting from one side and then to the other, looking out the window and then looking back to us, twirling her hair around her finger, and *telling* us how excited she was for the first two hours.

"Can you believe we're actually on our way?" she asked. "This is the best thing I've ever done in my whole life . . . I can't wait to get there. This is going to be so much fun."

"It better be," I said.

"What can you see out the window?" Greg asked her. He usually tried to change the subject whenever he thought I was being mean to her.

She looked out the window.

"A big river and a lot of square fields."

"How'd you get the window seat, anyway?" I asked, not quite ready to finish being mean.

She rolled her eyes and Greg elbowed me hard in the ribs.

"Do you want the window seat?" she asked.

"Maybe on the way home."

"What if Greg wants the window seat on the way home?"

"I'll stay right here," Greg said, settling his head against his seat. "I don't think you're supposed to move out of your assigned seats anyway."

"Why would it matter?" I asked.

65

"Because it's a lot easier for them to identify the bodies after a crash if everybody just stays strapped in their assigned seats."

Laci had never flown before either and we both glared at him. He grinned.

Eventually I leaned my head back and closed my eyes. I fell asleep, waking up when I heard Laci talking to Greg.

"What are you working on?"

"It's like a 'teach-yourself-physics' thing," he said, holding up a book. "Dad gave it to me."

"Don't you take physics when you're a senior?" I asked, rubbing my eyes.

"I'm going to take it when I'm a junior," he said. "I want to take AP Physics when I'm a senior so I can get some college credit before I get into the engineering program."

"What does an engineer do?" Laci asked. "I mean, I know you're not going to be driving a train . . ." she looked at me and smirked, "but what'll you be doing exactly . . . designing stuff?"

"Well, that's part of it," he said, "but there's a lot more to it than that. After you design something you build a prototype, or have someone else build it, and then you work with the prototype and you have to fix any problems and redesign it and make sure all the technical aspects are right."

"But," Laci said, "what are you going to be working on? Buildings? Cars?"

"I don't know yet. That's one of the great things about engineering . . ." he said. He was beginning to sound as excited about engineering as Laci was about Mexico. "You can work anywhere in the world and go into just about any field you want . . . aeronautical engineering, computer engineering, nuclear engineering, structural engineering, automotive engineering, cellular engin–"

"Okay, okay," I interrupted, putting my hand over his mouth. "We got it. You sound like Bubba on *Forrest Gump*. Boiled shrimp . . . fried shrimp . . . grilled shrimp . . ."

66

They both laughed.

"Did you say you're going to take physics as a junior?" I asked him.

He nodded.

"You can't do that unless you take Honors Geometry this year."

"I know."

"You signed up for *Honors?*"

He nodded again.

"That means you're going to have my mom," I said. "Good luck."

"You didn't sign up for Honors?" he asked, sounding disappointed.

"Nope."

"Why not? You did good last year in Algebra One."

"Why would I take Honors when I don't have to?" I asked.

"Well, first of all because it'll be fun to take it together and second of all because it'll look really good on your transcript. What are you going to major in?"

"I don't have any idea," I said. It was really starting to bother me that everybody else seemed to know what they wanted to do.

"You should go into engineering!"

I rolled my eyes.

"Oh come on!" he said. "I'll help you. We can go to State together and we'll be roommates – like Bert and Ernie."

"You watch too much TV with Charlotte," I told him.

"You can be Bert," he promised.

"Yeah, *right*," Laci murmured. "As if he could be Ernie."

We landed at the airport, picked up our luggage, and then waited for the bus to arrive. Another group of students from Pennsylvania was already waiting when we sat down. Everyone started chattering and laughing, excited about what lay ahead. Eventually an old white bus pulled up in front of us. The door opened up and a group of bedraggled teenagers filed out. They were dirty and appeared exhausted. They were also very, very quiet. We watched them trudge into the airport and then we picked up all of our things and climbed aboard.

It was dark by the time we dropped the Pennsylvania kids off at a church building on the outskirts of Mexico City. Our group was taken to a warehouse with no windows.

There was a corner reserved for us – the rest of the warehouse was filled with equipment and crates. The corner was partitioned off into two halves by cardboard walls – one side for the girls, and one side for the boys. Near the door was a drum of drinking water.

"Where's the hot tub?" I whispered to Laci. She jabbed an elbow into my side.

"Take water with you when you leave each morning," our group leader, Aaron was saying. "If you run out, wait until you get back here to drink."

He told us that he was from the United States and had been down here working for nine months. The organization was involved in many areas of Christian ministry to serve the poorest people of Mexico City. We would get to experience several of these areas. They usually had two or three church groups like us down here working every week, one group stepping in as another left.

On Monday we were going to the church where we had dropped off the Pennsylvania group. We would spend the day making improvements to the Sunday school classrooms and the outdoor play area. On Tuesday and Thursday we would go to a home-based church program that served children who lived in the landfill. The same bus that had picked us up today would go to the landfill, pick up children, and drive them to Philippe's house.

68

"Philippe," Aaron explained, "lives within walking distance of here with his wife. You'll also go there on Monday and Wednesday evenings to get prepared for the next day's activities."

On Wednesday and Friday we would go to a landfill and distribute food to the people who lived there. Saturday we would tour parts of Mexico City, distributing literature about the outreach programs offered by the organization. Sunday we would fly home.

We spread out our sleeping bags on the concrete floor and the next thing I knew we were being roused to go into the city.

The church where we had dropped off the Pennsylvania kids was in one of the poorer sections of town. The paint in the Sunday school classrooms had already been scraped and peeled and one of our jobs was to start rolling on paint. Mike and Greg and I went outside with Aaron to check out the playground equipment. Soon we were busy trying to erect a used swing set that had been donated to the church. The only problem was that it seemed to be composed of various parts from two or three different sets and none of them were compatible with each other.

Aaron told us that there was a hardware store around the corner and that we could go there if we needed to purchase something essential. We put our heads together, figured out what we needed, and then trekked to the store.

Unfortunately, the store was not set up like a typical American hardware store where customers were allowed to wander about, looking for what they needed. You were expected to tell the clerk what you wanted, and then he would go into the back and find it for you. He didn't speak a word of English.

"We're going to have to draw it out for him," I said.

"I can't draw," Mike said.

"Go for it," Greg told me.

I took a piece of paper and pencil from the man and drew out parts of the swing set, enlarging certain areas to elaborate with details about the parts we wanted. He came back with everything that we needed and soon we were on our way back to the church.

We started working on the set and found out that two of the parts we'd bought were not going to work the way we'd thought they would. I went back to the store and drew out some more descriptions, looking at the parts carefully before I took them to make sure they would work.

After we were finished, Greg looked at me and said, "Now, wasn't that fun?"

"I guess so," I said, suspiciously. "What's your point?"

"*That*," he said, "is what engineering is all about! You get to plan and draw and try something and if it doesn't work right you keep trying until you *make* it work right."

"So, what you're telling me is, if I go to State and room with you I can engineer swing sets?"

"Not unless you get into Honors Geometry."

That evening we went to Philippe's house and met Philippe and his wife, Teresita. They ran a home church for the poorest children in Mexico City. Every day except Sunday, a bus would bring about thirty kids to their home. I found it hard to believe that thirty children were going to fit in their tiny house.

"We always have students like you here to help us," Teresita explained. "You'll get to play with them, teach them some songs, and we feed them twice while they're here."

She spent the rest of the evening teaching us Spanish songs about Jesus and explaining to us what they meant. The children would all be little . . . under ten. She gave us some picture books in

Spanish with the story of Jesus spelled out phonetically. We practiced reading them aloud to each other.

Teresita showed us where the grocery supplies were and told us how we would need to prepare the food the next day. Meals would be given to the children first thing when they arrived and then again at the end of the day before they left.

"Children are much more likely to be able to hear and understand about Jesus' love for them if they're not busy thinking about how hungry they are," Teresita explained.

The next day we were spread throughout the tiny house – some of us in the kitchen, some in the bedroom, some in the living room, and some outside. When the bus pulled up a swarm of little children rushed toward the house, babbling excitedly in Spanish. They had never even met us before, but they hugged us and tugged at us, leading us toward the books, a CD player, and the food.

Greg and I were trying to read a story in Spanish to a small group of children when Laci walked by holding a little girl, about Charlotte's age, in her arms.

"This is Mercedes," Laci told us, hugging her close. "Isn't she the sweetest thing you've ever seen?"

They walked away, Mercedes chattering away animatedly to Laci in Spanish. Laci was smiling broadly. I think she was happier than I'd ever seen her before. Greg grinned at me and then we returned to reading aloud to our group.

On Wednesday we rode to the landfill. I was sitting next to Greg, absently flipping the metal toggle on the lid of my canteen, when I heard Greg say something under his breath.

"Oh, my God . . ."

I had *never* heard him take the Lord's name in vain before – *ever*. I lifted my head up and looked out the window that he was staring through.

We had arrived at the landfill.

It's difficult to describe what we saw, smelled and felt while we were there. The air was so heavy with putrid smells that our eyes burned for most of the day. Pigs were running around, stuffing their snouts into the piles of garbage, eating rotten fruit and meat. Two dogs, so skinny that their ribs seemed ready to jut through their mangy fur, fought over a dead rat. We saw a little boy pick up a bucket from Kentucky Fried Chicken and reach into it, pleased when he found a bone with some meat still on it. A white pipe ran up from the ground, water trickling from the top of it and forming a puddle on the ground. A young girl was collecting the drippings into the lid of a trashcan and washing her face and hands. She smiled at us as we pulled to a stop.

The children swarmed toward us at the sight of the bus, pouring out of shanties that were built on top of piles of garbage and made from cardboard and sheets of plastic. Some had constructed shelters from milk cartons, stacked and tied together with string or rope.

Mercedes appeared and ran toward Laci, hugging her and babbling in Spanish. Laci picked her up and led her to the back of the bus, where Ashlyn and Natalie were preparing to pass out food. The little girl who had been washing her hands and face ran up to Aaron, talking excitedly to him in Spanish.

"Quería verme bonita para los Americanos."

Aaron looked at us.

"She says she wanted to look pretty for you."

"You look very pretty," Greg told her.

"*Él dice que te ves muy bonita*," Aaron translated.

She beamed at us.

"*¿Por qué no vas al rededor del autobús a ver si hay algo para usted y su madre?*" Aaron said, pointing toward the bus.

The little girl smiled.

"*¡Está bien! ¡Espero que trajíste naranjas hoy!*" she shouted as she ran toward the back of the bus.

Aaron looked at us and smiled.

"She hopes we have oranges."

Greg and Mike and I each took a box of food and began traipsing through the dump, trying to reach the people who did not come up to the bus. Aaron had told us that some of them would not come because they were embarrassed at how they were living, while others were physically not able to travel even such a short distance. Either way, they all needed food.

When we had distributed all that we had, a boy about our age began gesturing to us and speaking in Spanish. Finally we understood that he wanted the empty boxes we had carried the food in. Aaron hadn't said anything about bringing the boxes back, so we nodded yes. He grinned and hobbled away to a shack nearby, tearing the boxes apart at the seams as he went. His feet were bare and we noticed that his right leg and foot were withered and bent.

We followed him. Greg stepped near a dead rat that was baking in the sun. Hundreds of flies erupted from its body.

We arrived at the boy's shack. He was attempting to replace a piece of rotting, battered poster board on the side of his shack with the new cardboard we had just given to him. We tried to help.

"It's not going to stay . . ." Greg said to us. "We could try to string it together with something, but . . ."

I looked around, but didn't see anything suitable.

"What if we could buy some vinyl clothes line?" Mike asked.

"Yeah," Greg said, nodding. "We could even pick up a tarp . . ."

"What about some sheet metal?" I suggested.

We all nodded.

"Uno momento," Greg told the boy, holding up one finger.

"Did that mean one minute?" Mike asked as we rushed back to Aaron with our plan.

"I hope so," Greg said.

We were certain that Aaron would drive us into town, but he just shook his head.

"It's not the best use of your time," he said.

"But we could build him something so much better," I protested. "We'll pay for it ourselves . . ."

He shook his head again.

"The government doesn't want them here," he explained. "These people build shacks at the landfill and the government bulldozes them down. They want these people to leave. Anything that you build for him will probably be destroyed in a few weeks."

He handed us some literature to share with the boy instead. It was the story of Jesus and Scripture verses and a prayer of salvation — all spelled out phonetically in Spanish, so that we could pronounce it and read it out loud to him. Aaron told us that he probably couldn't read.

We made our way back to the boy in his shack. He came out, smiling.

"I'm Greg," Greg said, tapping himself in the chest with a finger. He pointed at me, "David." Then at Mike, "Mike."

The boy grinned and repeated our names. Then he pointed at himself. "Miguel."

We sat down on some of the discarded poster board and tried to read the pamphlet out loud. Greg did a better job than either me or Mike, probably because Charlotte watched *Dora the Explorer* so much.

We joined hands with him and the three of us took turns praying for him in English. I know he didn't understand what we were saying, but he seemed pleased. When we were finished we walked back to the bus with tears in our eyes; the smell of the landfill was still stinging them.

In the evening we were leaving to walk over to do some more work at Philippe's house. Everyone loaded up their backpacks and filled their canteens with drinking water from the drum before heading out the warehouse door.

I was at the back of the group as we left the warehouse and I suddenly noticed – I don't know why – that Laci was not with us.

I went back into the warehouse, looking for her.

"Laci?" I called. She didn't answer, but I heard something from the girls' side of the cardboard wall.

"Laci?" I called again. I peeked my head around the cardboard. She was sitting on the floor with her head on bent knees, covering her eyes with her hands. Her shoulders were shaking and I knew she was crying.

"Hey, Laci," I said, walking over to her. "What's wrong?"

She just shook her head and didn't look up. I sloughed off my backpack and squatted down next to her.

"Laci," I said, shaking her shoulder gently. "Come on, Laci . . . what's wrong?"

She still didn't look at me, but she opened a hand and extended it in my direction. I picked up the dirty string and paper clip that she was holding.

"What's this?" I asked.

"A necklace," she said, wiping her eyes, trying to compose herself a bit. "A star necklace."

I examined it more closely. The paper clip had been bent into a shape that might pass for a star, and it was threaded onto the string.

"Why are you crying?"

"Mercedes gave it to me . . ." she said, starting to sob again.

I didn't say anything, but I sat down next to her and began rubbing her back.

"She has nothing . . . *nothing!*" Laci said. "And she gave me this and I can't do anything for her!"

"Come on, Laci," I said. "You are doing something for her–"

"What?" she asked, looking up at me with angry tears in her eyes. "What am I doing for her? Feeding her for four days out of her life?"

"Laci . . ."

"It's not enough!" she cried. "No matter what we do, it'll never be enough!

"And what's worse," she went on, "is that on Sunday we're going to get back onto a plane and go back to our houses and our TVs and our hot tubs and we're going to forget about all this."

"No we won't, Laci. We won't forget."

She wiped her eyes and glared at me.

"Yes, we will. You say we won't, but after we get home we'll feel differently. It won't ever feel like this again."

I didn't know what to say so I just kept rubbing her back.

"I don't know why God wanted me to come here," she finally said softly. "I thought we were going to do so much good . . ."

"We *have* done good," I said. "Don't say that. We've done *a lot* of good."

"It's not enough," she said again.

"You know that God didn't send you down here for no reason," I said. "You've got to look at the big picture . . ."

I wasn't sure at all what I was trying to say; as a matter of fact I was feeling pretty overwhelmed myself, but I didn't figure that was what she needed to hear right then.

"You mean, like maybe God's trying to show me something?"

"Maybe," I said. "I don't know."

She jumped on the idea.

"Maybe . . ." she said, her eyes beginning to shine, "maybe He's trying to show me what He wants me to do with my life!"

I saw the excitement growing on her face. I could picture her spending the rest of her life ministering to children in a landfill and trekking to the post office with an envelope full of hair every two or three years. I stopped rubbing her back and put my arm around her shoulder.

"Slow down, Laci. Don't go making any big decisions right now. All I'm saying is that you know very well that He sent you here for some reason and maybe if you just pray about it . . ."

She nodded and gave me a little smile, but I knew the wheels were already turning in her head.

"Do you think we should head over to Philippe's?" I asked.

She nodded and smiled again. We stood up, slung on our backpacks, and started out the door.

On Friday we went to the landfill again. This time, Mike and Greg and I all had our sleeping bags with us. We each took a box of food, set our sleeping bags on top, and trudged back into the landfill.

After the food had been distributed and the boxes contained only our sleeping bags, we found our way back to Miguel's shack. He wasn't there and I was disappointed.

"Do you think he'll be back soon?" Mike asked.

"I don't know," Greg said.

"Do you suppose it'll be okay if we do it anyway?" I asked.

"I really don't see how we can make things worse," Greg said, so we started.

We pulled the drawstrings out of the tops of our sleeping bags and from the stuff sacks and then we used them to tie the cardboard roof securely to the sides. The stuff sacks for my sleeping bag and for Mike's were waterproof, so we cut them apart at the seams and tied those across the top of the roof and secured them with the drawstrings too. Then we took apart the three cardboard boxes we'd carried the food in and spread them out on top of the garbage on the floor of the hut. We laid our sleeping bags on top of the cardboard and stepped back, admiring our work.

Miguel never showed up so we hiked back toward the bus with our hands empty.

"I wish we could have done more," Mike said.

"We did the most important thing . . ." Greg said, and I knew he was talking about reading to him and praying with him on Wednesday.

"I suppose," Mike said, "but we'll never see him again – we'll never even know if it did any good."

"Yes, we will," Greg said, "*one* day. One day we'll know."

~ ~ ~

OUR FRESHMAN YEAR of high school started three days after we got back from Mexico. On the first day of school I bumped into Laci at the guidance counselor's office. I was seeing if I could still get into Honors Geometry. Laci was there to drop French class and pick up Spanish.

"I'm already behind," she complained at youth group on Wednesday night. "I should have taken two years of Spanish in junior high."

"You'll be fine," Greg told her.

"I hope so," she said, doubtfully.

"Trust me, you will," Greg said.

I remembered that last year Laci had missed two weeks of school because she'd gotten sick with mono right before a major test in language arts. The teacher had berated the entire class afterwards because Laci did better than all of us and hadn't even been there for most of the material.

"Yeah," I agreed, "you'll do fine."

Mr. White wanted to move up with us into the senior high youth program so he and Mrs. Kelly switched and she moved down to work with the seventh and eighth graders. I'd expected Mike to complain about it, but while he and Laci and I were sitting on the curb waiting for our parents to pick us up, he talked enthusiastically about their plans for the year.

"And we're going on another mission trip next summer," he said. "I can't wait."

"Mr. White didn't say anything about that to us . . ." I said.

"That's because we don't get to go," Laci said, glumly.

79

"Why not?!"

"Because," she said. "The trip was really expensive, and they don't have enough money to pay for all the kids in church to go every year. They decided that in order to make it fair it would be a junior high thing only."

"I really wish you guys could come with us," Mike said, standing up because he saw his mom's car. As he said goodbye and headed away, I thought I'd never seen him so happy about being a grade behind me before.

"I wish *we* were going to get to go back," I said.

"Really?" Laci asked.

"Yes, really," I said. "Why do you sound so surprised?"

"I don't know," she said. "I guess I just always thought that you were mad at me because we didn't get to go skiing again."

I wondered if she really thought I was that shallow. Then I decided that since I'd always given her such a hard time about it, she probably did.

"No, Laci," I said, shaking my head. "As a matter of fact, I've been meaning to thank you for coming up with the idea. Going down there was really . . . it was really good."

"Do you mean that?" she asked, looking at me with bright eyes. I decided I needed to stop being mean to her.

"Yeah," I nodded. "And I also meant what I told you while we were down there . . . I'm not ever going to forget what it was like."

~ ~ ~

HONORS GEOMETRY WAS tough and Mom started to tutor me and Greg every Saturday afternoon. In addition to that, I found myself at lunch with Greg almost every day trying to work out problems or write a proof.

One day I put my head down on the cafeteria table, tired of trying to figure out what a contrapositive statement was.

"Why did I let you talk me into signing up for Honors?" I moaned.

"Come on," he said. "If you want to be an engineer you're going to need to get an A in this class."

Actually, I wasn't really sure that I wanted to be an engineer. I did want to go to State and I did want to room with him, but I had no idea what I truly wanted to do beyond that. Mom kept telling me not to worry about it . . . that lots of people didn't decide what they wanted to do until years after they'd graduated from college.

"Is that supposed to make me feel better?" I asked her, and she laughed.

"I'm just saying that it's okay not to know right now what you want to do. Do you like geometry?"

"Yeah," I admitted.

"Well, then just keep going in the subjects that you really enjoy and keep doing the best you can. You might not understand now what you're doing it for, but someday . . ."

"Do you have a graphing calculator?" Mom asked Greg one day as we sat at the dining room table with our geometry books in front of us. He shook his head.

"Hmmm," she said, rubbing her chin. "This section is going to be a lot easier with one . . ."

We had a class set at school, but we weren't allowed to bring them home. Mom had bought me one when I was in the seventh grade, but until Algebra One the only thing I'd used it for was to play games and write notes to Tanner or Greg in class.

As we sat at the kitchen table I found myself remembering the time that Mrs. Walsh had taken it away from us and Mom had to make a special trip to school to pick it up before Mrs. Walsh would give it back.

I didn't buy it for you to write notes! Mom had scolded on the way home. I was sulking in the seat next to her, mad at Tanner for getting us caught.

If you'd get me a phone we could just text each other.

You are not at school to socialize with your friends! she'd said, exasperated. *You're there to learn!*

"Dad can probably let me use one of the physics calculators," Greg was saying, bringing my mind back to our tutoring session. The science classrooms each had full sets too, but most of the kids in physics already had their own.

"One of the *many* benefits of having a parent who's a teacher," Mom said, raising an eyebrow at me.

"Oh, yeah . . ." I said, rolling my eyes. "So *many*, many benefits!"

Actually it wasn't so bad having her for a teacher. Sam was in Honors Geometry too and Mom had figured out pretty quick that I liked her. She enjoyed giving me a hard time about it, but when she rearranged our assigned seats I found myself sitting next to Sam.

"You're welcome," she said when we got into the car after school that day.

"I don't know what you're talking about," I said.

"Your grades had better not drop, young man," she continued, "or I'm moving you front and center and putting her in the back."

"I told you," I said, turning my head toward the window so that she wouldn't see me smile, "I don't know what you're talking about."

Greg and I were both on the JV soccer team, but Tanner, (who was quickly turning into a hulk) made varsity football. Greg and Mike and I all went to the games every Friday night to cheer him on. Being a freshman, he pulled a lot of bench time, but it was evident to everyone that he was going to be good in the years to come and Mike could hardly wait to join him. Sam, too, had made varsity as a freshman and watching her cheer at the games was another good reason to attend. I thought she was the best cheerleader that there was and that her place on the squad was well deserved. (I may have been slightly biased.)

Mrs. White taught our high school Sunday school class. Between her teaching Sunday school and Mr. White leading youth group, Mom complained that I was spending more time with Greg's parents than my own.

"Are they going to pay for your college tuition?" she wanted to know.

"I'll see what I can do," I told her.

After Thanksgiving break, swim practice began. We didn't have traditional "try-outs" like the other teams had. Instead, all the guys who wanted to swim trained together for over a month before swim meets started. Then – right before the first meet – Coach Covington would announce who'd made varsity.

The morning that he was going to make the announcement, Mom asked me if I was nervous.

"Not really," I shrugged. Nick was the only person who could beat me in the 100 butterfly and the 200 individual medley, and on a good day I could almost beat him.

"Well, good luck, honey," she said as I headed out the door.

That afternoon, when I came out of the locker room for practice to begin, I heard Charlotte's voice call out, "Davey!"

I looked up into the stands. There she was, with her parents and Greg and my parents and Tanner and Mike. They were all smiling and waving at me and when my name was announced for varsity they all clapped.

Who says swimmers don't have cheerleaders?

Soon it was February and I was at a Valentine's dance in the gymnasium. Greg had just finished dancing with Ashlyn when he walked up to me.

"Did that girl just ask you to dance?" he wanted to know.

I nodded.

"And let me guess . . . you told her '*no*'."

I nodded again.

"Have you suffered a recent head injury?" he asked.

"I don't even know her!" I protested.

He pinched the bridge of his nose and then rubbed his eyes.

"Listen," he finally said. "I'm sure that Sam finds it *terribly* attractive that you're standing here against a wall and everything, but maybe it would be a good idea for you to actually *dance* with someone while you're here. Whatdaya think?"

I sighed.

"If somebody else asks you to dance," he said, "do me a favor and say *yes*. Okay?"

I doubted that was going to happen so I nodded.

"I'll show ya how it's done," he grinned. He walked over to Laci, spoke to her, and then led her to the dance floor, looking over her head at me to smile. I rolled my eyes at him.

After I'd watched them dance for a minute I looked around. Sam was dancing with about the fifth guy I'd seen her with that night and Tanner was dancing with some junior. I decided that Greg was probably right. Even if Sam *had* noticed that I was here, she probably wasn't very impressed – I must have looked pretty pitiful. I made up my mind to dance with somebody before the night was over . . . even if I had to ask them myself.

Laci made it easy on me. As soon as she finished dancing with Greg she came over to me and asked me if I wanted to dance. She might as well have said: *Greg told me to come over here and ask you to dance because you're so pathetic* . . . but she didn't.

As I've said before, Laci is pretty and I didn't figure it would hurt anything for Sam to see me dancing with her, so I said yes.

It was a slow song and Laci put her arms around my neck and I put mine around her waist. I glanced around, looking for Sam, wanting to make sure that she knew I wasn't standing against a wall anymore, but I couldn't find her anywhere.

That figured.

"So how did Greg talk you into dancing with me?" I asked, turning my attention to Laci.

"He didn't," she said. "I wanted to dance with you."

"For a Christian girl you sure do lie well," I said, smiling.

"I'm not lying."

"Right. You're telling me that Greg had nothing to do with you coming over and asking me to dance?"

"I didn't say that," she admitted. "I just said that I wanted to dance with you."

"Well, anyway," I said, "thank you."

"Anytime."

"How's volleyball going?" I asked her.

"Not too great. We're three and eight so far."

"Ouch . . ." *That was pretty bad.*

"The swim team's been doing good though . . ." she said. "And I heard you beat Nick in the 100 fly last weekend."

I nodded and couldn't help but smile.

"Mr. White's helped me a lot," I said. "He showed me some strength training to do and he and Greg run with me about three times a week. I can really tell a difference."

"That's sweet of him," she said, "he's really nice. I hope I get him for chemistry."

"Jessica said he was really good," I said. "Even if I don't get him for chemistry next year I'm going to have him for physics in the eleventh grade and then for AP Physics when we're seniors."

"Are you going to have your mom again next year?"

"I'm not sure," I said. "I've got to take Honors Algebra Two and she doesn't usually teach that, so I'm probably going to have Mr. Hanover."

"So you're really going to be an engineer, huh?" she asked.

"I don't know," I admitted. "Mom told me not to worry about it too much right now and just take what I liked, so I guess that means math and science."

"I *hate* math," she said.

"You do?"

"I'm barely passing algebra," she said.

"Oh, come on," I said. "I don't believe that."

"Well," she admitted. "I'm passing, but it's my worst class. I'm barely making a B."

"What are you doing in there right now?" I asked.

"Slope-intercept or something like that," she shook her head. "I really don't have a clue."

"Oh, yeah," I said, "we just did that again in geometry."

"You have to learn it *again* in geometry?" She looked panicked.

"Well, yeah," I said, nodding. "You kind of keep using it over and over."

She shook her head. "I'm doomed."

"It's really not that hard . . . I bet I could explain it to you."

"I doubt it," she said.

"You're in first lunch, right?" I asked her. She nodded.

"Well, Greg and I are usually working on math all during lunch anyway. If you want I can try to show you on Monday."

"Really?" She sounded surprised – just like she had when I'd told her I was sorry we weren't going to go to Mexico again.

"Sure," I said.

"Thank you," she said. "I might do that."

The song was ending.

"No, thank *you*," I said. "It was nice dancing with you."

"Really?" she asked in that same tone.

"Laci," I said. "How come you always act like that?"

"Like what?"

"Like you can't believe I might actually say something nice and mean it?"

"I don't act like that," she said.

"Yes, you do!"

"No, I don't," she argued.

We still had our arms around each other and another song was starting.

"You wanna keep dancing?" I asked. She nodded.

"Anyway," I continued, "have I really been *that* awful to you?"

"I never said you were awful to me."

"I mean, I'll admit that I might not have been real nice to you when we were kids, and I may not be the most . . . the most *jovial* person in the world, but–"

She laughed.

"But, I've always thought that we were friends."

"We are . . ." she said.

"Remember how much fun we had ice fishing?"

She nodded and smiled.

"Come to think of it," I said, "you lied pretty good back then too."

"I told you," she said. "I wasn't lying."

I ignored her.

"And Mexico?" I said. "I mean, I would hope that after Mexico you would realize that I'm not so bad . . ."

"I never said that you were . . ."

"How's Spanish going, anyway?" I asked.

"*¡Tres bien!*"

"Good," I said, smiling and feeling forgiven for all the times I'd been mean to her.

"Are you going to Chicago in April?" she asked and I nodded. Mr. White was driving our church group to a youth rally over spring break.

"Skillet's going to be there," she said.

"I know," I nodded. "I can't wait to see them." I was excited about the hotel we would be staying at too because it had a heated pool and I was going to be able to work-out whenever I wanted – I didn't want to get out of shape once swim season was over.

We talked for a few more minutes until the song ended.

"Thanks again for asking me to dance," I said as we walked off the dance floor.

"You're welcome," she said.

"Don't forget about lunch on Monday, okay?" I reminded her.

"Okay."

I walked over to where Greg was standing, grinning at me.

"Well," he said, "you're still alive . . ."

"Oh, shut up."

"TWO songs? What were you talking about?"

"My hair," I said. "She was convincing me to start growing it out."

"Really?"

"No, not really, you dummy . . . we were talking about math. You and I are going to help her with algebra during lunch on Monday."

"You were talking about *math?*"

"Yeah . . ."

"Why would you talk to her about *math?*"

"What were you expecting me to talk to her about?"

"Well, Laci *is* a girl – in case you didn't notice. You could try to be nice to her."

"I was very nice to her," I said. "As a matter of fact, that's one of the things we talked about – what a nice guy I am."

"So, you didn't really just talk about math then?" he asked, looking pleased.

"I guess not," I said. "Why are you so concerned about what I was talking about with Laci, anyway? If you want to help me out, why don't you go convince *Sam* to dance with me?"

"Naw," he said, shaking his head and scanning the crowd, looking for someone to dance with. "I've done my good deed for the day. You're on your own now."

He loped off toward Natalie and I went back and leaned against my wall.

The dance had been on a Friday night. Saturday night it started snowing so hard that the plows couldn't keep up with it and by Sunday evening the announcement had been made that there would be no school on Monday. I called Greg.

"Wanna come over tomorrow?" I asked him.

"Um," he said. "Maybe you'd better come over here . . . my grandma's visiting."

"Oh," I said. "I don't want to intrude . . ."

"No, really . . ." he said. "Come on over. As a matter of fact . . . hang on for a second . . ."

I could hear talking in the background and then Greg said, "Are you there?"

"Yeah."

"Grandma said if you get here early enough she'll make you some of her famous waffles."

"Are you sure?"

"Sure, I'm sure," he said.

We usually had cold cereal at my house.

"I'll see you in the morning," I told him.

It was hard just walking the two blocks to Greg's house. Every now and then I'd come to a stretch where someone had already shoveled, but mostly I was in up to my knees.

"Come in, come in," Greg's mom said, pulling me in the door. "You must be freezing!"

"It's not that cold," I said, "but it's really deep."

"Will you help me build a snowman?" Charlotte asked, tugging on my arm.

"Absolutely," I said as Greg walked in the room. "A snow fort, too." I looked at Greg. "You've got a really deep drift over by that spruce tree in the front!"

"I know!" Greg said. "I've never seen this much snow before, have you?"

"A couple of times," I said, "but it's been a while."

We walked into the kitchen where Greg's dad and grandmother were.

"Good morning, Dave," Mr. White said. "You've met my mother before, right?"

"Of course we've met," she said, dismissing him with one hand.

"How are you David?" she asked, engulfing me in a big hug.

"Good," I said. "Thank you for inviting me to breakfast."

"Oh," she said. "You come over any time you want to!"

"He pretty much does that already," Greg's dad said. I glanced at him.

"Coffee?" he asked, grinning.

"Now don't you listen to him," Greg's grandmother said. "He's being a bad boy. You sit down right here and get ready to eat."

After breakfast Greg and I helped Charlotte get into a little pink snowsuit, matching cap, gloves and scarf.

"She looks like Ralphie's little brother on *A Christmas Story*," Greg commented and his mother and I laughed.

We went outside and started rolling up the bottom ball for our snowman. We both got a little carried away and soon it was huge.

"I want it over there," Charlotte said, pointing across the yard.

"I don't think we can push it any farther, Charlotte," I said. "It's too big."

She stuck her bottom lip out.

"Can you get a shovel?" I asked Greg.

He went to the garage and got one.

"She always gets her way," he complained as I whacked off the sides of the giant snowball.

"Just help me push," I grunted, tipping it over and heading toward where she'd been pointing.

"Is this where you want it?" Greg asked her. She nodded.

"Are you sure?" we both asked her and she nodded again.

"It's all lopsided now," Greg said.

"Well, you and Charlotte start packing snow on it to round it out and I'll start on the middle part, okay?"

"Okay."

I packed together a large snowball and started rolling it to the other side of the yard. I was just about to head back with it when I got hit in the face with a snowball.

"Oh, man!" I said, wiping snow out of my eyes. I got hit again and again and again – *hard*, and I knew that Greg couldn't be throwing that many at me all at once. I ran to the side of the house and peeked out. Laci and Mike and Tanner were all hiding behind the spruce tree, waiting to attack.

"This isn't fair!" I yelled. "It's three against one!"

"You've got Greg and Charlotte," Mike hollered back.

I looked over toward Greg. He and Charlotte were hiding behind the snowman's bottom.

"This isn't fair!" I yelled again.

"Okay, okay," Tanner called. "Truce . . . for now."

They dropped their snowballs and walked over to Greg and Charlotte while I pushed the middle of the snowman toward them. It was a good thing they'd arrived because Greg and I never would have been able to lift it up all by ourselves.

Mike rolled up a small one for the head and then Laci took Charlotte inside to look for a hat, scarf and face parts.

"Okay," I said. "Two on two now. Who do you want on your side, Greg?"

"Tanner." That was probably a good choice.

"Fine," I said. "Come on, Mike."

We ran over to the spruce tree and started stockpiling snowballs as fast as we could. Laci and Charlotte came out onto the front porch and sat on the steps, watching us fight. When we finally finished we helped Charlotte and Laci put the rest of the snowman together and then Greg's mom came out and took our picture with it.

"Come on in now and get warmed up," she said. "I made you some lunch."

I was still pretty full from the big breakfast I'd had, but I managed to eat a grilled cheese sandwich and a cup of clam chowder soup. I was tipping my cup up when I noticed Laci looking at me.

"What?" I asked.

"It's Monday," she replied.

"So?"

"So . . . it's *lunch* on *Monday*."

"Oh!" I said, wiping my mouth. "You really want to work on it now?"

"No," she answered, laughing. "I was just kidding."

"We can if you want to. I don't mind."

"Gee, I'd *love* to," she said, "but I didn't bring my textbook."

"It's online."

"Oh."

Soon we were sitting in the White's office looking at her Algebra One textbook online. I printed out a page of problems and set them in front of her.

"Here," I said, tapping at the paper. "Try number thirteen."

"I don't even have a clue where to start," she said.

"Get y by itself."

"Why do you do that?"

"So that you can get it in slope-intercept form," I said.

"How do you know what slope-intercept form is?" she asked.

"You just have to memorize that," I said. "But for right now, just get y by itself. Do you know how to do that?"

"I think so," she said. She leaned over her paper and worked for a little while, but I couldn't see what she was doing because her hair was really long (stage three) and it was covering up all of her work.

"Nobody's going to cheat off you in class, are they?" I asked.

"Am I doing that bad?"

"I have no idea," I said. "I can't see anything you're doing."

"Oh!" she said, sitting up. She pulled a rubber band out of a cup on Mr. White's desk and pulled her hair back into it.

"Isn't it getting about time for another donation?" I asked her.

"Pretty quick," she said, nodding. "But I like it to be long enough so that I don't have to get it cut too short. I wouldn't want to look like a *boy*, you know."

She looked me square in the eye and raised her eyebrow when she said the word '*boy*'.

"Laci, that was like, FOUR years ago!! I told you I was sorry for being mean to you when we were little."

"No, you didn't," she argued.

"Yes I did," I said.

"When?"

"When we were dancing . . ."

"No, you didn't," she said again.

I tried to think back to our conversation. I was pretty sure that I'd told her I was sorry . . .

"Are you sure?"

"Yes," she nodded. "I'm sure."

I finally decided that if she wanted an apology that badly she probably would have noticed if she'd gotten one.

"Well then," I said. "I'm very sorry, and I wish you could just forget about it."

"If you help me get an A in algebra I'll never think about it again," she promised.

Mr. White walked into the office and took a book off the shelf.

"What are you two working on?" he asked, looking at Laci's paper. "*Oooh!* Slope-intercept! That's always fun!"

"Oh, yeah," Laci rolled her eyes. "So much fun."

"Oh, stop it," I said, picking up her paper. I looked it over, relieved that she at least knew how to solve for *y*. Mr. White patted her on the back.

"Okay," I said. "Good. Now all you've got to do is graph it."

"Fun, fun, fun," she sighed.

Laci knew a whole lot more than she thought she did and we got through the entire section in less than an hour. I was showing her how to take practice quizzes online when Mike, Tanner, Greg and Charlotte came in.

"Tanner and I are gonna get going, Laci," Mike said. "I promised my mom I'd shovel the driveway and the sidewalks before it gets dark. Do you want us to walk you home?"

"Please don't leave yet, Laci," Charlotte begged, grabbing her arm. "You haven't played with me all afternoon."

"I guess I can stay a little while longer," she told Charlotte, and Charlotte hugged her.

We finished the practice quiz and I showed her a couple other things she could do at home. Then we put our snow gear back on and went outside.

Charlotte and Greg were working on a snow fort. We built two of them and then had a snowball fight . . . me and Charlotte against Greg and Laci. They lobbed them gently at Charlotte, but whenever they got a clear shot of me they really let loose. Finally I got smart and loaded Charlotte up with a snowball in each hand. I held her up in front of my face and raced toward Greg and Laci. They threw snowballs at my legs and when we were right in front of them I yelled, "Now, Charlotte! NOW!" She hit them both and I retreated, running backwards, still holding Charlotte in front of my face.

After the snowball fight Laci helped Charlotte make snow angels.

"That was really low," Greg said as we sat on the porch and watched them. "Using a small, innocent child as a shield."

Greg's mother poked her head out the door.

"Laci?" she called. "Do you want to stay for lasagna? I already called your mother and she said it was alright with her if you wanted to."

"Thank you!" Laci said, nodding.

I looked up at Mrs. White and stuck my bottom lip out at her just like Charlotte had done to us that morning.

"Get that look off your face," she smiled at me. "Your mother said 'yes', too."

"I heard you went to Collens College," Laci said to Greg's grandmother over dinner. "That's where I'm thinking about going."

"It's a *wonderful* school!" she said. "You should definitely go, you'll love it."

I held off on the "small women" jokes.

"How'd you wind up in Florida?" Laci asked her.

"You kids may think it's fun to build snowmen and throw snowballs now, but just wait 'til you're my age. You'll be heading south as soon as the leaves start changing color."

"Don't you miss the snow?" I asked her.

"Nope," she said, shaking her head. "The only way I'm coming back here to live is if all the nursing homes in Florida are full when I'm ninety."

"We've got a really good nursing home here," I smiled.

"Yeah," Greg agreed. "It's not too far from the animal shelter . . ."

"DON'T you guys even start!" Laci said, putting her fork down and glaring at us.

"Are they being mean to you, Laci?" Greg's grandmother asked. Laci nodded and Greg and I both started laughing.

"Shame on you both," his grandmother scolded, shaking a finger at us. "You shouldn't be mean to her – Laci's a very sweet girl. One day the two of you will probably be fighting over her."

Obviously she hadn't met Sam.

"Yours wouldn't be the first friendship to break up over a pretty girl," she continued. She wagged her finger at me and then at Greg. "You be nice to Laci."

We both nodded at her and smiled and I decided to change the subject.

"This is the best lasagna you've ever made," I told Greg's mom. I saw Greg's dad bite his lip and then shake his head.

"What?" I asked him.

He nodded toward Greg's grandmother who was beaming.

"It's very good," Greg's mom agreed. "But Greg's *grandmother* made it."

"Oh!" I said. "Well, really it's about the same as–"

"STOP!" Mr. White interrupted me. "You have entered into a land where no man should ever have to set foot. You *cannot* win. Nothing you say will be right. *Nothing.*"

"But–"

"Uh, uh, uh!" he said, shaking a finger at me. "Stop talking. Stop right now. Just sit quietly and eat your lasagna. Don't say another word."

Laci and Greg were both stifling laughs.

"I was just going to offer to do the dishes after supper," I said quietly, looking down at my plate and trying not to smile.

Greg and I walked Laci home after supper. Laci was in the middle and we were shoulder to shoulder because, even though most of the sidewalks had been shoveled during the day, they were narrower than usual.

"Hey, Greg," I said, hooking my arm into Laci's and pulling her close to me. "Should we just go ahead and start fighting over Laci now?"

"We can share her if you want," he suggested, doing the same thing to her other arm. "I'd hate to bust up such a good friendship just over some girl."

"That's a good idea," I nodded. "What do you think, Laci? Do you want to be our girl?"

She lifted her chin up high, trying not to smile.

"You'll see," she said, shaking her hair out behind her. "One day the guys will be lining up around the block just *waiting* to see me."

"I'm surprised they aren't already," Greg told her and she grinned at him.

From then on we called her "our girl" and Greg made up a hand signal for it. Whenever the three of us were together he would catch her eye, point at her, and then wave his finger back and forth between himself and me. *You're our girl.* She always smiled when he did it. She also started eating lunch with us every day, whether she needed help in algebra or not.

About a week before the youth rally in Chicago, Laci bounded up to our table.

"How's our girl doing?" I asked. She held up an algebra test with a "99" at the top. Greg gave her a high five.

"What'd ya miss?" I asked, snatching it from her.

"Number four," she said. I put down my fork and started working the problem out.

"That's right," I said. "How come he counted it wrong?"

"He thought I wrote thirteen point four instead of thirteen point nine. I didn't make my nine clearly."

"That's obviously a *nine*," I said. "Anyone can tell that's a nine. This should be a hundred. You should go back to him and see if you can get him to give you a hundred."

"Oh, relax, David," she said. "This is great! It's the best grade I've ever made in there. One point doesn't matter."

"It does too matter!" I said, picking my fork back up. "I worked hard for that grade."

She laughed and shook her head.

"I think you should go back and try to get him to change it," I said again.

"And I think," she said, "that you should quit being such a grump!"

~ ~ ~

IT WAS A five-hour trip to Chicago and the three of us sat next to each other in the new church van, singing along with the radio the entire way – I knew the songs as well as anybody else.

The hotel was very nice, (not as nice as the ski lodge had been, but very nice) and I was not unhappy to find a hot tub next to the swimming pool. The first evening we went to the Skillet concert which was as great as I'd expected it to be. The next day we broke into small groups in different conference rooms, depending on which session we had signed up for ahead of time.

During lunch there was a performance by a group of students with disabilities. I think most of them were mentally challenged, but some of them were blind or deaf. They were all dressed in white robes with red collars and they had white gloves on their hands. In front of each one of them was a bell. Their director pointed at each one of them when she wanted them to ring their bell. If a student was blind, someone standing next to them would tell them when to ring their bell. The music they made was absolutely *unbelievable* – I hadn't thought anything could top Skillet.

In the afternoon we broke up for more sessions in conference rooms. Greg and I had both signed up for one together called "Being a Christian Athlete" which *I* thought was going to be about being a Christian athlete.

"You're a real idiot, you know that?" Greg said when I told him that.

"What's it going to be about then?" I asked.

"You know," he said. "Running with patience the race that is set before us . . . fighting the good fight . . . faithfully running the course?"

"Oh."

Of course he was right, but it was still really good and mostly guys had signed up for it, so I figured I wasn't the only one who had misunderstood what it was going to be about.

I had never really noticed before how many references there were in the Bible that compared staying faithful to Christ with competing in an athletic event. The session leader told us that winners of races back then were awarded a crown of leaves. Even though they were evergreen they would eventually wither and die.

"But," he said, "we're told in Corinthians that the crown we obtain as Christians is incorruptible."

At the end of the session we were shown pictures of Derek Redmond, a British runner who had competed in the 1992 Olympics in Barcelona, Spain.

We saw pictures of him training, competing and winning all of his qualifying heats. Then – with 250 meters out of 400 to go in his semifinal heat – we saw pictures of him falling, then getting up, trying to finish his race.

He had torn his hamstring, but he continued down the track, hopping on one leg, crying, and trying to finish. His father somehow got past security and ran out onto the track, putting his arm around his son and helping him to make it across the finish line.

"You've *got* to finish the race," the session leader told us. "And sometimes you can't do it alone. That's why it's vitally important that you make Christian friends . . . that you have others who will help you when you stumble and fall."

Greg looked at me and smiled and I smiled back and I really did appreciate that we would be there for each other. But sitting there in that conference room that day in Chicago, I felt so right with God that I honestly could not imagine that there might come a time when I would stumble and fall.

That night we had free time, so of course I went to the pool. Greg and Laci were sitting in the hot tub talking when I finished doing laps. I sat down on the edge of the hot tub and put my feet in.

"Wow . . . that's hot!" I said.

"Not after you've been in for a while," Laci said.

"Laci and I were just talking . . ." Greg grinned.

"Uh-oh," I said. "This can't be good."

"Oh, stop it!" She splashed a handful of water at me.

"What were you talking about?"

"Oh, Laci was just saying that we're spending A LOT of money here at this hotel and that maybe next year . . ."

"Oh, come *on*, Laci!" I said. "I just texted Mike and told him how great this was and how we couldn't wait for him to come with us next year!"

"I know," she said, "I've had fun too, but . . ."

"As I was telling Laci," Greg interrupted, "sometimes it's okay for Christians to get together and have fun, even if it costs money."

"Yeah," I said. "It's called *fellowship!*"

"Plus," Greg continued, "it's really good for us to come someplace like this and hear these speakers and be together."

"It just seems sinful to be spending so much money," she said quietly.

"Laci," I said, lowering myself on to the next step in the hot tub. "You can't feel guilty every time you spend some money or have some fun."

She looked at me uncertainly.

"Now look," I said. "I'll be the first to admit that I could get used to this very easily. But *honestly?* If God told me to give it all up? I would. He's just not telling me that. He's telling me that this is where He wants me right now. It's bringing everybody closer to each other and closer to Him – that's important too.

"Well put," Greg nodded.

"Thank you . . . I have my moments."

102

"Yeah!" Laci said, smiling. "Especially when it involves making sure you get some hot tub time every year!"

"I'm not telling you what you should do," I continued, dropping down into the water so that I was finally at the same level with them, "but every time you see someone having fun or spending money, you can't just say that they shouldn't be doing that."

"That's right," Greg agreed.

"You must think that I sound really . . . self-righteous," she said.

"No," Greg said seriously, "not at all."

"Laci," I said, shaking my head, "you have *never* been self-righteous."

"And we think it's very sweet," Greg added, "that you want to run off and save the entire world – *right this very second*. That's why you're our girl."

They smiled at each other and then she glanced at me. I nodded at her and smiled too.

"Thanks," she said.

After the youth rally, the three of us became particularly close. Maybe there was a bond between us because we all put God first in our lives and we knew that about each other and we respected it and we were willing to share that with each other. Maybe it was because we had done so many things together that a strong friendship had developed. Probably it was a combination of both.

Whatever the reason, it was something that all of us realized was happening, and that just brought us closer still.

~ ~ ~

THE FIRST WEEK of summer vacation Greg went to Florida to visit his grandmother like he did every year. Tuesday morning I had just finished working out at the pool and was floating lazily on my back when I saw Tanner waving a hand at me. I popped up and started treading water.

"What's up?" I asked, but he just knelt by the edge of the pool and motioned for me to swim over to him. I could tell by the look on his face that something was wrong.

When I got there I put my arms on the edge of the pool and looked up at him.

"Mike's dad died," Tanner said.

I looked at him for another moment and then laid my head on my arm against the edge of the pool and closed my eyes.

The visitation was on Thursday night and the funeral was on Friday. The funeral home had a large chapel and Mike and his mom and both sets of his grandparents were there. Jessica was home from her freshman year at State for summer vacation and we all stood in line together.

I embraced Mike's mom and told her how sorry I was, and then introduced myself to his grandparents. They had met me years before, but I'd changed a lot since then. When I got to Mike I couldn't say anything, so I just gave him a big hug.

It was an open casket and I had never seen a dead person before. It was an eerie experience. Mike's dad looked gaunt and waxy, yet he didn't look dead. It seemed as if he were only sleeping and I kept expecting him to twitch or move.

The casket top was split in half and the part covering his legs and feet was closed. I could see things tucked down in there: a teddy bear . . . a picture of him holding Mike as a toddler . . . a model rocket . . . a can of his favorite soda . . . a pocket watch.

"How do they stand there and talk to all those people without crying?" Jessica asked on the ride home.

"They've probably spent the last three days crying," Dad told her.

"Everybody reacts differently when they lose someone," Mom said. "I remember when my father died . . ."

I had never met my grandfather on my mom's side. He had died before my parents were even married.

"I was home from college for Christmas break," she went on. "He had a heart attack and died before the ambulance could even get there. It was just such a . . . such a *shock*. It didn't seem real.

"It was as if I was in a fog for the entire three days before the funeral. I didn't cry at all. I really don't even remember much about the funeral. The only thing I really do remember is that when I got home, I headed to my room to change out of my black dress. I was going up the stairs and I just . . . I just collapsed on the steps and started crying and crying. I lost it. I just completely broke down and lost it."

We rode in silence for a few moments.

"I hope Mike's okay," I finally said.

After the funeral the next day we were invited to Mike's house. There were a lot of people there – cars were lined up and down the block and the funeral home had posted signs along the curbs: *Please drive slowly . . . death in family.*

Mike lived three blocks from us. We walked.

Everyone who came brought food – my mom and Jessica brought deviled eggs and strawberries. It was like a party. Not a loud party, but a party.

The doorbell rang. Mike's mother was standing near me and she asked me if I could get it. I opened the door. It was Laci.

As soon as she saw me she burst into tears. I grabbed her arm and wheeled her back around. I closed the door behind me and we sat down on the steps.

"I'm sorry," she sobbed. "I just feel so bad for Mike and his mom." I didn't say anything; I just sat there and rubbed her back like I had in Mexico. After a minute, the front door opened again and I looked behind me. It was Mike. He looked at Laci and then at me and he gave me a small, sad smile and shook his head. He sat down on the other side of her. I let him take over rubbing her back.

"It's okay, Laci," he said softly.

She looked up at him and flung her arms around his neck.

"I'm so sorry, Mike," she cried.

"I know," he said, hugging her back. "Thank you."

"Are you okay?" she asked him

"I am," he nodded.

"How's your mom?"

"We're doing fine. We've had a long time to get ready for this."

Laci looked at him.

"Don't get me wrong," he said. "I'm going to miss him-"

His eyes filled with tears.

"But," he went on, "Dad was so sick . . . for so long. He was ready to go and he knew where he was going. He wasn't afraid to die. That makes it a lot easier."

Laci nodded.

"Are you okay?" he asked her. She nodded again.

"We've got a video we're going to show with pictures of him when he was little, and Mom and Dad's wedding and stuff," Mike said. "Do you want to come in?"

"All right," Laci said, and we all stood up and went inside.

The next week Greg returned from Florida. When I got out of the pool he was sitting in a lounge chair waiting for me. I let him know what had happened.

"How's Mike doing?" he asked, obviously concerned.

I told him about the conversation he'd had with me and Laci on the steps.

"I think he's alright," I said. "He went to football training camp with Tanner this week."

"Well, that's good."

"How was Florida?" I asked.

He shrugged. "It was okay, I guess."

"You don't sound very enthusiastic . . . what happened? You were so excited about going . . ."

"I don't know," he said. "It's just different every time I go back there."

"How so?"

"It was just different with my old friends, you know? We've all changed so much and . . . I don't know. Things just weren't like they were before."

"Weren't they glad to see you?"

"Oh, yeah," he said, "and we went out and did stuff and everything, but . . . I don't know how to explain it. It was just different."

"Oh . . ."

"You should come down there with me next year," he said.

"Yeah, right."

"No," he said, sitting up on one elbow. "I'm serious. I already asked Mom and Dad and they said if it was all right with your parents it was okay with them."

"For real?"

"Yeah, for real. I think they felt sorry for me because I was moping around. You know – kind of like you do all the time."

I let that pass.

"Wow . . . Florida!"

"So I take it you want to go?"

I'd never even been out of the Central Time Zone before.

"Oh yeah!" I said. "I wanna go!"

We didn't see Mike and Tanner too much over the summer. The football coach saw to it that the weight room was kept open and they were both expected to take advantage of it. In addition to the training camp that they'd gone to right after Mike's dad died, they had another one at State that lasted for five days and a two-week-long training at the high school itself. Football was pretty big in Cavendish.

Laci and Greg, on the other hand, apparently had *nothing* to do. They were usually both there by the time I finished swimming laps in the morning. We hung out together most days, swimming, playing pool and wasting our money on video games and pinball machines.

"You're getting a job next summer," my mom said one day, handing me money as I walked out the door.

"You'd better get me a car then," I said. "So I can get back and forth to work."

"We'll worry about that after you get your driver's license."

"Only eight more months!" I grinned.

"Don't remind me," she said.

The next day I noticed a poster on the bulletin board at the pool for lifeguard certification classes.

I walked up to Josh, one of the lifeguards on duty, who was usually there in the mornings when I worked out.

"Hey, Josh!"

"Hey, David. What's up?"

"How hard do you think it would be for me to get a job here next summer?"

"You thinkin' about getting certified?" he asked.

I nodded.

"Just apply really early . . . like in March. I don't think you'll have any problem. I can put in a good word with the manager for you if you want me to."

It didn't take me long to decide that it would be a perfect job so I nodded and said thanks. Before I left that day I jotted down the number and called that night to sign up for the classes.

Mom wasn't thrilled when she had to start driving me to the YMCA three times a week. Every time she complained about it though I reminded her that it was *her* idea for me to get a job next summer.

"You should be proud of me that I'm planning so far in advance," I told her.

"I am, David," she said, smiling. "I've always been very proud of you. I'm also glad that you're planning on getting a job that you can get to on your bike."

"I'm never going to get a car," I moaned.

"Not if I can help it," she agreed, still smiling.

Not surprisingly, Mike made the football team with Tanner in the fall. Greg and Laci and I always sat together at the games to cheer them on, and Natalie and Ashlyn usually joined us. After the

Homecoming Game the seven of us went to the Homecoming Dance. I danced with Laci and Natalie and Ashlyn and when some girl I didn't even know asked me to dance I said yes.

I don't know if Sam was impressed or not, but at least Greg seemed pleased.

I was in Algebra Two and chemistry and although I did pretty good I had to work awfully hard and that helped keep my mind off of Sam . . . *sort of*. I didn't have any classes with her this year, but I still kept my eye on her in the hall or across the lunchroom.

My sophomore year was the only time that Tanner and Mike and Greg and I all had the same lunch together. Laci and Natalie and Ashlyn all had it too and we sat together almost every day. Greg and I usually had our heads stuck in a book while the rest of them talked.

"I hope you two aren't taking your school work with you to Chicago," Laci said. We were scheduled to go to the youth rally again over spring break. "You're no fun when you're working all the time."

"Math *is* fun," I reminded her and she rolled her eyes at me.

"By the way," Mike said. "I'm not going with you guys in the spring."

"Why not?" five of us asked at the same time.

"I'm going to the Bahamas!"

We all stared at him.

"My mom and I are taking a cruise," he explained.

"Life is so unfair," Tanner said, resting his cheek on his hand.

"What are you doing over spring break?" Natalie asked him.

"I imagine I'll be playing video games with my little brothers," he said.

"I'll send you a postcard," Mike said, grinning.

"Gee," Tanner said, narrowing his eyes at him. "Thanks."

"Don't worry," Greg said. "We'll send you one too."

"Wow!" Tanner said as he plastered a huge, fake smile on his face. "You guys are just the greatest."

110

Natalie and Ashlyn wound up not going with us to Chicago either because Natalie's family went to Denver to visit relatives and they invited Ashlyn to go along. It was too bad they couldn't all come because the rally was as good as it had been the year before.

On the second day, after lunch, I was sitting between Laci and Greg, listening to a speaker. He was young – probably in his early twenties – and he was talking to us about how important it was for us to show Christian love to each other.

"Love is one of the central themes of the Bible," he was saying, "and we all know that we are called to love one another. But how often do we really let our fellow Christians *know* that we love them?

"We should be hearing Christians say 'I love you' to each other on a *regular* basis . . ." He held up his hand in the universal "I love you" signal – pinkie finger, pointer finger and thumb up . . . ring finger and middle finger down. He turned from one side of the audience to the other, showing us his hand. "We should be seeing Christians, holding up this sign to one another on a *regular* basis . . ."

Now, *knowing* how much Greg liked hand signals I should have guessed what was coming next. But I didn't.

He looked at Laci and gave her the sign. She did it right back and smiled at him. Then he gave it to me.

"Oh, no you don't!" I said, shaking my head at him.

"What?" he asked innocently.

"NO! You are not flashing me an 'I love you' sign at school. You can just get that out of your head right now!"

"Why not?"

"Because everybody'll think we're *gay*, you moron!"

"You mean you're not?"

I smacked him (hard) and Laci burst out laughing.

"Oh, come on," he chided. "Weren't you listening to what he was saying?"

"Yes, I was listening to what he was saying, and now I want you to listen to what *I'm* saying. Under *no* circumstances are you to *ever* flash me the 'I love you' sign. Do you understand?"

He honestly looked a bit hurt.

"Besides," I said, hoping to placate him a little, "all your hand signals are *secret*, remember? You don't want everybody else knowing what you're saying . . . do you?"

His face brightened. "What if I do something else?"

I rolled my eyes.

"How 'bout this?"

He pointed to his eye. "I." He pointed to his heart. "Love." Then he pointed at me. "You!"

"Get away from me, you long-haired, hippy-freak."

Laci laughed again.

"Okay. No, seriously," he said. "What if I make up something different so that no one else would know?"

"Maybe," I conceded. "It depends on what you come up with."

"I could give you the bird," he grinned.

"That would be good," I nodded. "Instead of killing two birds with one stone I could express two feelings with one bird." I wasn't smiling, but they both were.

"I'll help you come up with something that won't embarrass old grumpy here," Laci offered, poking me in the ribs. Greg nodded at her.

"I have to approve of it first," I said, "and if either of you ever tell anybody what it means, I'll never speak to you again. *Understand?*"

They both nodded at me solemnly and then flashed me the "I love you" sign before they started laughing.

They took their new task quite seriously. Laci came over to our room that evening to help Greg come up with an idea. I went into

112

the bathroom to change into my bathing suit and when I came out, they were both sitting on his bed with their heads bent together.

"Go away," Laci said when she caught me listening to them. "You're going to be lucky if we even share our signal with you."

"Don't worry," I said, heading out the door. "I'm going swimming."

"We'll miss you!" Greg called after me.

I'd done forty-two lengths when Laci's hand appeared underwater, waving to me from the end of the lane. I stood up and took off my goggles.

"What?" I said as if I was not happy to have my workout disturbed. Actually, I was so out of shape that my muscles were throbbing and I was just about to quit anyway.

Both of them were squatting down beside the pool, twisting the straight index finger of one hand into the palm of the other. They both had huge grins on their faces.

While I ran my hands over my face to get the water out of my eyes I decided that no one would ever be able to figure out what it meant.

"Okay," I said, looking up at them. "Tell me about it."

Greg held up his index finger. "This is a nail," he said. He pushed it into the palm of his other hand and twisted it back and forth. "Christ loved us so much that He died for us-"

Laci went on. "That's how much we're supposed to love each other."

I looked down at my hands and twisted my index finger into my palm.

"I love it," I said, looking up at them and grinning back. "It's perfect."

"Yeah," Greg agreed. "It's better than the bird."

~ ~ ~

THE WEEK AFTER we got back from the rally I turned sixteen. I got to go to any restaurant I wanted to for dinner that night and I'd picked *Hunter's*.

"I cannot *believe* this is where you wanted to come," Jessica said, pulling off a slice of pizza.

"This is my favorite place."

"Now, Jessica," Dad said. "Leave David alone."

I think I was his favorite child right then. We'd gone to *Chez Condrez* for Jessica's sixteenth birthday and it had cost Dad about a hundred and twenty-five bucks.

"I wouldn't have driven all the way home if I'd known this is where we were going to eat," she complained.

"Two hours, Jess," I said. "*Big deal.* You should be willing to drive twenty hours just to wish me a happy birthday."

"Yeah," she said, "and almost get killed on the ride to the restaurant."

"We didn't almost get killed."

"I also can't believe they gave you a driver's license," she muttered.

"Hey, look!" Greg said. We were eating so cheap that I'd asked Mom and Dad if he could come with us. "They've got a 'Help Wanted' sign up!"

"I don't know why you don't get certified and lifeguard with me," I told him.

"Because I want something I can keep doing after school starts. Besides that, I bet if I work here I can get you an employee discount!"

"Aren't you guys going to Florida right after school gets out?" Jessica asked.

"Yup!" I said, grinning.

114

"Isn't the pool going to be kinda mad when you miss the whole first week of work?" she asked me.

"I told them about it during the interview," I explained. "They said we could work around it."

Three weeks later Greg started his new job.

"I can't believe they don't make you wear a hairnet," I said. Greg's ponytail was hanging out the back of a cap that said: *Hunter's Pizza and Subs.*

"That's why I like working here," he answered. "They don't make me wash my hands after I go to the bathroom either."

He handed my sub over the counter.

"Enjoy."

I smirked at him and took a bite.

"Has Laci found a job yet?" Greg asked.

"Yfs, su dot," I nodded. "Sfs gft un jsb nt kndys."

"How's that sub?" he asked, raising an eyebrow at me.

"Sf ghoud," I said, nodding again.

He waited for me to swallow.

"So *what's* she doing?"

"She's going to be working at Kennedy's."

"That men's clothing store in the mall?"

"Yep," I said.

"Just for the summer?"

"She's not sure," I said. "That's when they're busiest – renting tuxes for weddings and stuff – but she might stay on part-time after school starts again."

"When does she start?" Greg asked.

"Next week."

"What about you?"

"The day after we get back from Florida," I said.

I could hardly wait.

~ ~ ~

SUMMER ARRIVED QUICKLY and the day after school ended I flew to Florida with Greg's family. I got to sit next to the window on the plane. Greg's grandmother was waiting for us at the airport.

"Oh, Charlotte!" she said. "How's my baby?" She squatted down next to Charlotte and they gave each other a big hug.

"Look what I got for you for graduating from kindergarten!" she said. She held out a shirt that matched her own . . . it was turquoise with blue and pink butterflies.

"Greg!" she said, reaching up to hug him because he was taller than she was now. "How's my favorite grandson?" He was her only grandson.

I got hugged next.

"David! How's my other favorite grandson?"

She had t-shirts for both of us too. Greg's was green with a white sea turtle on the back. Mine was a washed-out red with a white logo on the chest pocket. The logo was a cross with the word "Lifeguard" above it, and "Tarpon Springs, Fla." underneath. I liked it a lot and was especially glad that Greg and I didn't wind up with matching shirts.

Greg's grandmother lived in Crystal Beach, about five miles south of Tarpon Springs. Her house was small with only two bedrooms. Greg's parents would get the extra bedroom and Charlotte and Greg and I were going to sleep in the living room – one of us on the couch, one of us on an Aerobed, and one of us in a sleeping bag on the floor.

"I'll sleep on the floor," I offered, feeling very honored that I'd been invited along at all.

Charlotte's eyes filled up with tears and she began wailing. "*I* wanted to sleep on the floor! *I* wanted to sleep on the floor!"

116

I got the couch.

Greg's grandmother had a gas log fireplace (I couldn't imagine when she ever needed it) and a mantle covered with framed photos. I studied them while Greg was blowing up his Aerobed.

"Who's this?" I asked, showing him a picture of a boy about ten years old who was holding a baby. "That's not you and Charlotte . . . *is it?*"

He looked up at it and nodded. "Yup."

"Man, I can't believe that's you!" I said. His hair was in a crew cut and blond . . . almost white. He was wearing shorts and his skin was dark brown.

"I know," he said. "I'm just as pale as you now."

"I'm going to get a tan while I'm down here," I told him.

"You'd better wear sunscreen while you're down here."

I looked at another picture. I could tell that it was a young Mr. and Mrs. White, faces pressed together, smiling with goggles and ski hats and gloves. White snow was in the background.

There was an eight by ten school photo of Greg . . . probably taken in about the first or second grade. Tucked in the corner of the frame was a picture of me and Greg and Laci, smiling and sitting at the picnic table at Cross Lake with playing cards in front of us.

"Hey!" I said. "I'm up here too!"

"You've made the big time now," Greg acknowledged, unplugging the Aerobed cord. "My grandma's mantle."

"I can't believe I am swimming in the Gulf of Mexico," I told Greg as we bobbed up and down in the waves. "This is so cool. Hey! Look at that!"

A nearby boat was pulling a parasail.

"I got to do that once," Greg said. "It was pretty neat. You're flying above everybody and you can see sharks in the water and stuff."

"Sharks?"

"Yeah," he said. "You look down and there's people swimming with sharks right around 'em and they don't even know it . . ."

"You're kidding, right?"

"Oh, brother," he said, rolling his eyes. "Most of them are only like . . . this big." He held his hands about two feet apart.

"You're serious? There're sharks around here?"

"Well, this *is* part of the Atlantic ocean . . ."

"I'm getting out . . ." I said, starting to fight the waves to get to shore. Then I stepped on something.

"There's something down there!" I said, trying to keep my feet off the bottom.

"Sand, maybe?" Greg asked.

"No, I'm serious," I said, "something weird."

"It's probably just a shark."

"You're *not* funny!" I said, tentatively putting a foot down again. "Oh! There's another one!"

Greg dunked his head under the water and emerged a few seconds later with something in his hand.

"This maybe?" he asked, extending his arm to me.

I looked at it, hesitantly.

"What is that?" I asked.

"It's just a sand dollar."

"It doesn't look like a sand dollar," I said, taking it from him. It was brown and velvety. "How come it's not all smooth and white?"

"Because it's still alive," Greg explained, and I almost dropped it. "When they harvest them they lay them out in the sun and when they die all these little hairs fall off and they turn white."

I looked carefully. All the little hairs were moving, trying to make it go somewhere. I tossed it gently into deeper water and went under,

118

feeling around on the floor bottom until I found two more. I popped up with them.

"Look! I caught sand dollars!" I said.

"Are you going to keep them?" Greg asked.

"No, I'm going to let them go," I said. "They're cool though!"

"That's about the millionth time you've said 'cool' since we got here yesterday," Greg smiled.

"Oh, right. Like you didn't do the same thing after you moved to Cavendish," I said. "Cool . . . snow! Cool . . . an icicle! Cool . . . a snowdrift! Cool . . . sleet!"

"Cool!" he said, pointing behind me. "A shark!"

"Very funny!" I answered, *knowing* that he was only kidding, yet still having to turn around anyway. I took a few involuntary steps back toward the shore, trying not to crush any sand dollars.

The next day we went to another beach. I was really grateful that Charlotte was around so that I had an excuse for catching sand fleas, collecting shells and making drip castles (which I was pretty much an expert at by now). Greg tolerated my second childhood fairly well.

"Do you think you can tear yourself away from the beach for the day tomorrow?" he asked.

"Probably," I said. "Why?"

"I thought we'd get together with some of my old friends and do some biking on the Pinellas trail."

"Sounds like a plan."

We had a great time with Greg's old friends and although they were very nice (I had not really expected otherwise), I understood why Greg had wanted me to come to Florida with him. It was natural for his friends to talk about things that had happened recently, about things that Greg didn't know anything about, or to make jokes that only they got. Likewise, when we stopped at an arcade to play pool and Greg clawed his hand through the air, they didn't know why I laughed.

When Greg said goodbye to them at the end of the day and told them he'd see them next year, I found myself feeling very thankful for my friends and my life in Cavendish. I was glad that no one was going to move . . . nothing was going to change.

Two days before we were scheduled to fly home we went to the aquarium in Tarpon Springs. They had a touch tank where you could pet and feed stingrays and nurse sharks. I made Charlotte go with me and I stood there amongst a bunch of little kids running my hand across slimy stingrays until a shark finally got close enough for me to touch.

"I touched a shark!" I told the Whites when I met them at the alligator exhibit. They all smiled and at the gift shop I bought two shark–tooth key rings (one for Tanner and one for Mike) and two shark–tooth necklaces (one for Laci and one for Jessica).

We went out to eat that night at a restaurant called *Mama's Greek Cuisine*. Greg's grandmother told me that Tarpon Springs had a higher percentage of Greek-Americans than any other city in the United States.

"They came here with their families as sponge divers around the turn of the century," she explained. "Then in 1947, a red tide wiped out almost all of the sponges."

The waitress came and took our drink orders.

"Anyway," Greg's grandmother continued, "the sponge industry never really recovered from that, but Tarpon Springs is still famous for its sponges."

"I never even knew there was such a thing as a *sponge industry*," I said.

Greg nodded.

"We'll walk around the sponge docks after dinner," he said. "You'll see."

I started looking at my menu.

"Smelt?" I said. "They serve smelt here?"

"What's wrong with smelt?" Greg asked.

"Nothing, I guess," I said, "but I'm not going to order something I can catch in Lake Michigan. I want something special – something that I can't get around home. What's calamari?"

"Squid," Mr. White said.

"And I think you can get that at home if you'd just go someplace to eat besides *Hunter's*," Greg told me. "You should get *spanakopita* or *dolmades*." His parents and grandmother nodded in agreement.

"What are '*dolmades*'?" I asked.

"Right here," Greg said, pointing at the menu. "Ground beef and rice wrapped in grape leaves and topped with an egg-lemon sauce."

"*Grape leaves?*"

"Do you want me to see if they have hot dogs?" Greg asked.

"No," I said. "I'm going to be adventurous. What's the other thing you said?"

"*Spanakopita*," Greg's grandmother said. "It's spinach pie with layers of phyllo dough and feta cheese."

"Spinach?"

Greg rolled his eyes.

"No, no . . ." I said, holding up a hand. "I'm going to get one of them . . . I just can't decide."

"How about if I get one and you get the other and we can split 'em," Greg suggested.

I nodded. I also ordered broiled octopus as an appetizer and baklava for dessert.

After supper we walked around the sponge docks, investigating the gift shops that were packed along the Anclote River. I was in line holding two sponges when Greg walked up to me.

"What are you getting those for?"

"For my mom and dad," I said, holding them up. "Genuine sponges from Tarpon Springs."

"Give me those," he muttered under his breath. He took them from me and threw them back into a bin. "Let's go.

"Those sponges aren't from here," he explained when we got outside. "That place is just a tourist trap."

"Where are they from?"

"Imported from overseas somewhere," he said. "Come on."

We walked about two blocks until we came to the Tarpon Sponge Company. Greg assured me that the sponges were locally harvested. I bought four.

On our last evening we were sitting on the beach, waiting for the sun to set over the Gulf of Mexico. I was thinking to myself about the gifts that I was taking home with me. Suddenly I looked at Greg.

"What?" he asked.

"I . . . I didn't get you anything . . . to thank you for bringing me down here."

"Wanna know what you can do to thank me?" he asked.

I nodded.

"Come back next year," he smiled.

"Are you serious?"

"Sure," he said. "We can make it an annual thing . . . one day we'll bring our wives and kids."

I smiled back at him.

"You've got a deal!"

We sat there quietly for a few minutes and I let myself imagine leaving my kids with Greg and his wife while Sam and I took a walk on the beach.

"You know what's over there?" Greg asked, pointing slightly south and interrupting my thoughts.

"Mexico?"

"Yeah," he said.

"Do you think about it a lot?" I asked him.

"Yeah," he nodded, glancing at me. "Do you?"

"Every day."

"Do you think you'll ever go back there?"

"I don't really want to," I admitted. "That probably sounds terrible, doesn't it?"

"No," he said. "I know exactly what you mean."

"It would be easier just to get rich and write a check and let somebody else do it."

"Another good reason to be an engineer," he said with a smile.

"Don't get me wrong," I told him. "If I'm supposed to go back . . . I will."

"I know," he answered quietly. We both sat in silence and watched the sun drop below the waves.

~ ~ ~

MY NEW JOB was fun. I loved sitting in my lifeguard chair, twirling my whistle, ordering people to stop building pyramids and telling little kids not to run. Like the summer before, Greg and Laci came by almost every day, and we usually played pool or swam during my breaks.

One day Sam showed up as the guest of a member. She spotted me in my chair and came over.

"Hey, David!" she said. "I didn't know you were a lifeguard!"

"Yeah," I said. "How are you doing?"

"Good," she said. "Are you having a good summer?"

"It's been great. How 'bout you?"

"Pretty good," she said. "Have you had to save anybody yet?"

"Not really," I answered, deciding that getting a bag of ice for the kid who'd cracked his lip open on the diving board didn't really count.

"You ready for school to start?"

"Not really," I said again.

"Are you taking statistics this fall?"

"No." I shook my head, quickly trying to figure out if I could fit that into my schedule somehow. "Pre-calc."

"Oh," she answered, sounding disappointed. "Well, maybe we'll get to take something else together this year."

"That would be good," I nodded.

"Well," she said. "My friends are waiting, I'd better go. See ya around!"

"Yeah," I said, "see ya."

I turned my attention back to the pool and glanced around quickly, relieved not to find anybody floating face down in the water.

I wound up having one class with Sam during our junior year – American History.

When I'd signed up for my fall classes, in addition to American History and Pre-Calculus and Physics, I had decided to take a class called Life Skills. It was designed to help us do things like set goals, organize our time, and develop better study skills. When I walked into the room on the first day of school I noticed that the wall was covered with motivational posters like: IF YOU FAIL TO PLAN, PLAN TO FAIL, and IF YOU DON'T KNOW WHERE YOU ARE GOING, YOU'RE NEVER GOING TO GET THERE. I figured it would be an easy A.

The first thing our teacher had us do was to envision ourselves at some point in the future. She said it didn't matter if it was ten months from now or ten years from now, just to picture ourselves in the future doing something that we hoped to be doing. She turned off the lights and made us put our heads down on our desks so that we could concentrate.

I imagined myself nine months from now at the Junior/Senior Prom with Sam. We were slow dancing and she was *definitely* my girlfriend. It was a great daydream and I was sorely disappointed when the teacher turned the lights back on.

"Now," she said, passing out composition notebooks to each of us, "I want you to write down what you envisioned – what it is that you want to be doing in the future."

Yeah, right . . . like I was going to write that down.

She wrote on the board, GOAL.

"What you saw yourself doing . . . that is your goal," she said. "Write this down in your composition notebooks. It's very important that you write it in positive terms and in present tense. Your mind will not like for you to say something that is not true. If you keep saying something that is not true, your subconscious mind will begin working to either make you quit saying it or to make what you are saying true. If you persist and keep saying it, your mind will figure out a way to help you achieve your goal. You get what you focus on.

"Don't ever begin a goal with the words 'I will not . . .' – you want the goal to be expressed in positive terms, like this: 'I have lost ten pounds,' or 'I am making straight A's'. Write your goal in your composition book now."

Someone raised their hand.

"Can it be two sentences?"

"You can make it two sentences if you have to, but it's better to make your goal as concise as possible."

I wrote: GOAL – *I am on the Dean's List at State.* (Jessica always made the Dean's List and Mom and Dad seemed pretty happy about it.)

In my *mind* though, I wrote: GOAL – *I am dancing at the prom with my girlfriend, Sam.*

"Next," the teacher said, "you need to write a specific time frame to achieve your goal. Your goal must be measurable in time. For example, maybe you want to lose ten pounds by December, or perhaps you want to make straight A's by the end of the spring semester.

In my composition notebook I wrote: *Each semester at college.*

In my mind I wrote: *April.*

"Now," she continued. "You need to write down at least three steps, three things that you can do, that will help you achieve your goal. For example, if I wanted to lose ten pounds by December then I would need to perhaps exercise four times a week for an hour each time, increase the number of leafy green vegetables I eat to five servings a day, and eliminate all sugar products from my diet. Think about three things that will help you to achieve your goal. Don't forget to write these in positive terms as well."

In my notebook I wrote:

1) *Spend two hours each night studying for my classes.*

2) *Complete all major assignments at least one week before they are due.*

126

3) *Keep my notes and handouts organized.*

I looked up. The teacher was standing behind me, reading over my shoulder what I had written. She smiled at me and gave me a nod of approval.

I smiled back at her and in my mind I wrote:

1) *Ask Sam to dance with me at the Homecoming Dance.*

2) *Give Sam a Christmas present.*

3) *Ask Sam out on a date.*

"Okay, class," she said as she walked back to the front of the room. "Now to make this goal a reality, you need to focus on it. Each day you need to state your goal to yourself in positive terms. Say it over and over to yourself. Remember, you get what you focus on. Set that goal in the forefront of your mind. Keep that vision right there where you can see it. Picture yourself, achieving your goal, over and over. '*I have lost ten pounds . . . I have lost ten pounds*'. Picture it.

"If you commit to doing this and *make* yourself take the steps that you've listed, your mind is going to help you figure out a way to make your goal a reality. Everybody practice now. Close your eyes. Concentrate. Say it to yourself and picture it."

I am dancing at the prom with my girlfriend, Sam. I am dancing at the prom with my girlfriend, Sam. I closed my eyes and saw myself at the prom in the spring with Sam. We were slow dancing and I was holding her close. She was my girlfriend.

"Can you do that, class? Are you willing to do what's necessary to achieve your goal?"

I opened my eyes. She was scanning the class, searching for affirmation. When she looked at me I nodded at her and smiled. I could do that. No problem.

A few weeks later I was at Kennedy's in the mall with Greg, looking for a suit for my cousin's wedding in New York. I was going to get to miss school on Friday. We went on an afternoon when Laci was working so she could give me her employee discount. Mom told me to get the suit a little too big in case I needed it again in the next year or so.

"You're so lucky you're going to New York," Greg said.

"Yes, that's me," I replied. "Lucky, lucky, lucky."

"What's your problem now?" he asked.

The Homecoming Dance was only two weeks away and I had promised myself I was going to ask Sam to dance. I was already starting to get worried about it.

"Nothing," I muttered. "Hey! Look at that!" I pointed at a leather jacket on a mannequin. "I wonder how mad Mom would be if I bought that instead of a suit."

"Um . . . I'm thinking pretty mad," Greg said.

I looked at the price tag on the jacket.

"Wow! Never mind . . . I don't have enough money anyway."

Laci walked up to us.

"Hey, Laci!" I said. "What kind of a deal can you cut me on this jacket?"

"I thought you were here to buy a suit."

"I am, but just think how good I'd look in that jacket."

She smiled at me.

"Let's see," she said, taking it off the mannequin and handing it to me.

"Feel this!" I said to Greg, shoving it at him.

"It's lovely," he said.

I put it on and looked at myself in the three-way mirror.

"Now THAT," I smiled, "is one fine-looking man."

Laci laughed.

"*Joo lewk mah-vah-lous!*" Greg agreed. I took it off reluctantly and handed it back to Laci.

"Can you hold it for me?" I asked her.

"Until when?" she asked.

"Until he's a rich engineer," Greg said.

"Yeah," I nodded. "I'm thinking about six years."

"Sorry," she said, smiling and putting it back on the mannequin.

We walked over to the suits and started looking for my size, but I found myself glancing back at the leather jacket. All I could think was that I bet Sam would notice me if I showed up somewhere wearing that.

By the time the Homecoming Dance rolled around I was a nervous wreck. Like we did at every game, Laci and Greg and I sat together to cheer Tanner and Mike on. All through the game I kept watching Sam cheer and I practiced asking her to dance in my mind. When Mike recovered the other team's fumble and made a touchdown, I completely missed the whole play.

At the dance I danced with Laci and a few other friends – anything to put off asking Sam – but when I finally noticed the DJ's wife beginning to wind up extension cords I knew I was running out of time. I forced myself to walk over to her.

I am dancing at the prom with my girlfriend, Sam. I am dancing at the prom with my girlfriend, Sam.

"Hi, Sam," I said as the last slow song of the evening started to play. "Do you want to dance?"

"I'd love to," she said, taking my hand. I swallowed hard and led her to the dance floor. I was shaking and hoped she wouldn't notice. She put her arms around my neck and I put mine around her waist and then she moved closer to me and laid her head on my shoulder. I could smell her hair. It smelled like suntan lotion and I inhaled deeply, thinking that, if I could just stay there forever – smelling suntan lotion and holding her – I would never need anything else again.

When the song ended I had stopped shaking and was feeling quite proud of myself. Life Skills was my favorite, *favorite* class and the smell of suntan lotion was the greatest scent in the world.

Mom and Dad had let me take the car and when I gave Greg a lift home I told him all about my dance with Sam in vivid detail. He didn't seem as happy for me as I'd expected, but he didn't call me grumpy a single time during the entire ride home.

The next thing I needed to do was buy Sam a Christmas present. I started shopping in early November, knowing that I would buy her a bracelet, but wanting it to be the perfect one. She wore bracelets *a lot* and I watched them dangle from her wrist as she passed notes back and forth to Angel in history. The week after the Homecoming Dance, a tightly folded note had landed on my desk and I read it after class, locked in a stall in the bathroom:

David -
I'm going to the movies with some friends Saturday night - You should come too!
♡ luv, Sam

Luv Sam.

LUV Sam . . .

I caught her by her locker after school.

"What time are you going to the movies?" I asked her.

"Seven-thirty," she said. "Are you coming?"

"I'll try," I nodded and she smiled.

The movie experience was not all I had hoped for. I didn't get to smell her hair or even sit close to her because there were about five other people with her and somehow I got separated from her when everyone was deciding where to sit. The experience was, however, satisfying enough that I could barely tell Mom anything about the movie when I got home.

I bought her not only a bracelet, but matching earrings and a necklace. I wasn't sure what I was doing, so I made Jessica come along with me when she was home for Thanksgiving.

"Are you sure?" I asked her.

"She'll love them."

"Are you *sure*?" I asked again. "This is really important, Jess."

"Yes," she said, "I'm sure. They're very pretty. There's no way she's not going to like them. Relax."

"Why does everybody always tell me to relax?" I asked.

"Because," she told me, "you need to relax!"

"Easier said than done," I said and I headed to the counter to pay for them before I could change my mind.

I waited until the last minute to give them to her. The bell rang, dismissing us for Christmas break. I was waiting for her when she got to her locker.

"Hi, David," she said, smiling at me.

"Hi, Sam," I said. I was nervous, but I don't think I was shaking. "I have something for you . . ."

I handed her the package.

"Oh, David! That's so sweet!" she said. "Should I open it now or wait until Christmas?"

"You can open it now," I said, and she did.

"Oh, my God!! I love them. They're beautiful!" I was looking at her smile, trying to make sure she really liked them, when she kissed me suddenly on the lips. "Thank you!" she said, still smiling.

"You're welcome," I said. "Merry Christmas!"

Jessica was coming home tomorrow. I walked to the bus, smiling and thinking that I was going to tell her that she had really, really *great* taste in jewelry.

~ ~ ~

CHRISTMAS OF MY junior year in high school was the best I ever had. It started when I pulled a tiny box from under our tree and opened a set of keys. With Mom and Dad and Jessica following I ran out into the garage and laid eyes on my first car. It was sporty enough that I loved it, but it was also loaded with enough safety features to ease Mom's mind.

"Can I go show Greg?" I begged.

"Go ahead," Mom sighed.

Despite how excited I was, I remembered to grab Greg's present before I left. I'd bought him a subscription to *Popular Science* and Mrs. White had snuck the first issue to me before Greg saw it. It was wrapped up in a shirt box with a gift subscription card. I knew his dad was going to love it too and I was pretty proud of myself. I even had a stuffed bear for Charlotte.

I bounded up the brick steps and rang the doorbell. Charlotte answered the door, still in her pajamas, and threw her arms around my knees.

"Merry Christmas, David!"

"Hey, Charlotte!" I said, handing her the bear. She hugged me again and ran off to show her parents.

Greg was sitting on the floor in front of the tree trying to take one of Charlotte's toys out of its box. It was fastened in with a variety of clips and screws and he was working with a screwdriver, a knife, and a pair of scissors.

"Merry Christmas!" I said, tossing the shirt box at him.

"Thanks," he said, taking the box "but if this is going to be hard to open I don't think I want it."

"Naw," I replied, flopping down on the couch. "I wrapped it myself. You're lucky it didn't fall open already."

He opened it up, took out the magazine and read the card. I could tell that he liked it.

"Thanks," he said. "Dad'll like it too."

"That's what I figured," I said. I had my keys around my finger and was twirling them.

He *finally* noticed.

"No way!"

"Yep!" I knew I was grinning like Cheshire cat.

"Are you serious?" he asked.

"Come see for yourself!"

We went out into the driveway and he gave the car all the proper respect it deserved.

"Go get your coat on," I said, "I might even let you drive."

"Hang on," he replied and ran into the house.

When he came back out he had a large package with him.

"Here," he said, handing it to me.

"Thanks!" I ripped the paper off and opened the box. I couldn't believe my eyes. It was the leather jacket we'd seen at the mall when I'd bought my suit for the wedding.

"Oh, man . . . you didn't have to do this," I said.

"Yeah, I know," he was smiling. I couldn't imagine how many hours he'd had to work to pay for it even with any discounts Laci might have been able to get him.

"I can't accept this."

"You have to," he said. "There was this huge sale . . . no exchanges, no returns."

"Liar."

"Try it on."

I did.

"Is it too big?" He looked worried.

"No," I said, "it's perfect. Hopefully I'm still growing and I'm going to want to wear this *forever*. It's perfect. Thank you."

He seemed genuinely pleased.

134

To show my appreciation, I let him drive first. That gave me a chance to examine the console and glove compartment of my new car and the pockets of my new jacket.

"I don't think I've ever seen you smile so much," Greg said, glancing at me.

"I'm not having a bad day," I admitted. "Keep your eyes on the road."

"Where do you want to go?" he asked.

"Let's drive by Sam's house."

"Really?"

"Sure! I bet I could knock on her door and ask her to marry me and she'd take one look at my new jacket and my new car and she'd throw herself into my arms."

He waved a hand at me dismissively and he shook his head. "You don't want to marry her."

"Keep both hands on the wheel," I said. "How do you know? I might want to marry her."

"Naw," he shook his head. "She's not the one for you."

"What are you talking about?" I thought about the kiss she'd given me in the hall. "Sam and I are getting close."

With that he burst out laughing.

"No, you're not, man. You and Sam are never going to be close."

"Yes we are!" I argued.

"You know what I should have bought you for Christmas?" he asked.

"What?"

"A telescope," he said. When I didn't say anything he went on. "You know why?"

I had a feeling I didn't want to know.

"Why?" I finally asked.

"Because you and Sam are so far apart that you need a telescope to see her." With that remark he formed his fingers into a tube and held them up to his eye as if he was peering through a telescope.

"Very funny," I replied. "Keep both hands on the wheel."

"I'm serious, David," he said. "She's not the one for you."

"Why would you say that?" I asked, hearing the anger begin to creep into my voice.

"Because," he hesitated, his voice growing serious, "her heart's not like yours."

"Her heart's just fine!" I told him, wondering why he was trying to ruin such a perfect day. "You hardly even know her!"

"Look. I'm sorry. I didn't want to make you mad. I just," he shrugged, "I just don't think she's the one for you, that's all."

"Okay, then, smarty," I said. "Who *is* the one for me?"

"Laci."

"*Laci?!*"

"Yeah," he said. "Laci."

"What are you talking about?"

"I mean *Laci*," he said. "Laci's the one for you."

"Laci's just a friend."

"She could be more."

"No," I said, shaking my head. "I love Laci, you know that. Laci's great . . . but we're just friends."

"You should ask her out some time," he suggested. "Just see how things go."

"Why don't *you* ask her out?" I said.

"Because she doesn't like me," he answered.

"Yes she does!"

"No she doesn't. Not that way."

"Well," I said, "she doesn't like *me* that way either."

He slowed the car and pulled it over to the side of the road. He turned the engine off and looked at me.

"Yes, she does."

It was very, very quiet in my new car.

Finally I spoke. "Are you sure?"

"Yes," he said, nodding his head. "I'm sure."

I thought for a minute, trying to digest what he was telling me.

"What am I going to do?" I finally blurted. "I don't want to hurt Laci . . ."

"Then don't . . ."

"But I like *Sam!*"

He held his hand up to his eye again, giving me the telescope signal, and then he looked at me.

"It's your turn to drive," he said, and he dropped the keys into my hand.

~ ~ ~

THE NEXT FEW months were ... *awkward*. For over four years I'd had a crush on Sam and those feelings weren't about to just suddenly go away – especially now that she was finally showing interest in me. Laci acted exactly the same as she always had and I realized that she didn't know that I knew.

I asked Sam out on an official date, and when that went well, I asked her to the prom, but what I'd told Greg was true; I didn't want to hurt Laci. When Sam and I walked down the hall together I would drop her hand if I saw Laci coming.

Fortunately, things got less awkward one day at lunch.

"Tanner asked me to the prom," Laci said. Sam and I had different lunch periods so I still ate with Laci and Greg almost every day.

"Are you serious?" I asked.

She nodded.

"Are you going?" Greg asked her.

She nodded again.

"That's fantastic!" I said, grinning. If she liked Tanner I could quit worrying about hurting her feelings and concentrate on Sam.

"Why are you so happy?" she asked.

"Because," I said. "Tanner's one of my best friends ... you're one of my best friends ... I think it'd be great if you two were a couple."

"I didn't say we were a *couple!*" she protested. "I just said we're going to the prom together. We're friends."

"Right!" I nodded. But when I saw Tanner and Laci walking down the hall together and laughing the next day, I didn't bother dropping Sam's hand.

Greg, on the other hand, didn't seem as pleased. He cornered me after physics class the next week.

"Did I see Sam walking down the hall wearing my jacket?" he asked.

"*My* jacket," I corrected him.

"I didn't buy it for her, you know!"

"I bet you wouldn't care if *Laci* was wearing it!" I said.

"Probably not," he admitted, "but that's just because Laci's the one."

"Oh, stop saying that and stop telling me that Sam and I are so far apart." He'd been giving me the telescope signal every chance he got.

"You were wrong," I said, "okay? Laci's *not* the one. She's going to the prom with Tanner . . . I'm going to the prom with Sam . . . you were *wrong*! Why don't you worry about finding yourself a date for the prom?"

"I already have a date for the prom, thank you very much."

"You're kidding! Who'd want to go to the prom with a long-haired, hippie-freak like you?"

"Natalie . . ."

"Really?"

"Yup," he said.

"Well, good," I replied, nodding my approval and patting him on the shoulder. "Now why don't you go find Natalie and quit worrying about me and Sam and your jacket, okay?"

"Nope. Can't do it," he said, holding up his telescope. "Laci's the one."

Sam and I only had one fight, and I'm not really sure that it even qualified as a fight. On a day that I knew Laci wasn't working, Sam and I had gone to Kennedy's to rent my tux. We were looking through a catalogue to find a tie and vest that would match her dress. She called it champagne, but it just looked gold to me.

"Oh my God!!" she said, pointing at one of the pictures. "That would look so good on you!"

"I wish you'd quit saying that," I told her.

"Saying what?"

"Oh my God!"

She looked at me. "Why?"

"Because," I said, "it's taking the Lord's name in vain . . . you know . . . one of the top ten things you're not supposed to do?!"

"No it's not," she said.

"Yes it is," I argued.

"No," she said. "Taking the Lord's name in vain is when you say 'Oh, Jesus Christ' or 'G.D.' or something like that."

I shook my head. "You shouldn't say 'Oh my God!' either."

She looked at me for a moment – I think to see if I was serious – and she must have decided that I was.

"Good Lord," she said, rolling her eyes at me, and then she walked away to get another catalogue.

Prom night came and I picked Sam up at her house. Her mother let me in and called Sam. She came down the stairs in her champagne dress looking more beautiful than I had ever seen her. Her hair was curled in loose ringlets and they cascaded all around her shoulders.

"Your hair looks fantastic," I said. She smiled at me.

"Thank you. I hope you won't be disappointed on Monday when it's straight again. This is too much work for every day."

"Don't worry," I said. "Straight's good too."

I pinned her corsage on, we posed so her parents could take a bunch of pictures, and then we got in my car.

140

"Where are we going for dinner?" she asked.

"It's still a surprise," I told her. I was taking her to *Chez Condrez,* the restaurant Jessica had picked for her sixteenth birthday.

When the escargot arrived she wrinkled up her nose.

"I didn't know they would still be in their little shells," she said. "They look so cute."

I hadn't known they'd be in their little shells either, but I also didn't know if I would have described them as cute. *Gross,* maybe, but not cute.

"We've got to eat them," I said. "They cost fifteen dollars!"

"You first," she insisted, spearing one on a fork and holding it in front of my mouth. I figured that since I'd eaten broiled octopus, I could eat a snail. I opened my mouth and took it off the fork, chewing only once and then swallowing. It was a lot spicier than I'd been expecting.

"It's not bad," I said, getting one for her. "Your turn."

"Promise it's not bad?"

"I promise."

She gathered up all her hair in one hand and held it to one side of her head as if it were in a ponytail. She opened her mouth and took the escargot, chewing it thoughtfully. I looked at the bundle of hair hanging from her hand and all of a sudden I wondered how many inches long it was and how a little girl would look with a wig made from that hair.

"David?" she was saying. "David, did you hear me?"

I blinked and looked back at her face.

"What?"

"I said you were right . . . it isn't bad," she said. "What were you thinking about just then?"

"Oh," I said, shaking my head. "Just your hair. I was just thinking how much I like your hair."

By the time we arrived at the prom, most of the tables were taken and the dance floor was full. We finally found two seats and had just sat down when a slow song started and Sam grabbed my hand.

"Oh my God!" she said, tugging me toward the floor. "I love this song . . . come on!"

As I held her close, I suddenly appreciated that I had achieved the goal I'd set for myself in Life Skills on the first day of the school year.

I am dancing at the prom with my girlfriend, Sam. I am dancing at the prom with my girlfriend, Sam.

I'd done exactly what I'd promised myself I would do and I had what I'd told myself I wanted . . .

The funny thing was that I wasn't as *happy* as I'd thought I'd be.

I pulled Sam closer and rested my cheek on the top of her head, smelling that suntan lotion scent that had mesmerized me at the Homecoming Dance. We continued dancing and I thought about Sam saying that she loved this song. I realized that I had never even heard it before. A vague feeling of discontentment settled over me.

What's wrong with me? I thought. *I've got everything I've ever wanted . . . why can't I just enjoy it and be happy?*

And then Greg's voice answered me in my head.

Her heart's not like yours . . .

It sounded as clear as it had on Christmas day when we'd been driving around in my new car. It sounded *so* clear, in fact, that I actually thought he'd said it out loud and I glanced around looking for him, thinking that he and Natalie must be dancing somewhere near us.

I couldn't find them. I only saw Tanner . . . holding Laci against his large frame as they danced. I watched them for a long moment and then Tanner saw me looking at them and he smiled at me and nodded his head. I managed to smile and nod my head back, but I felt my discontentment grow. I turned away and rested my cheek back on Sam's head and continued dancing.

~ ~ ~

AFTER THE PROM I found myself watching Tanner and Laci a *lot*. I couldn't tell if they were dating or if they were just the same good friends that they'd always been, but every time I saw them laughing together or saw him rest his hand on her shoulder, something inside of me would stir. I tried to deny the feeling that was smoldering inside of me, but eventually I had to admit to myself that it was envy – growing and making me angry at each of them. I started to avoid them both.

If there'd ever been a time to call me grumpy, it would have been then, but even Greg was sensitive enough not to joke about it.

Just before exam week, Sam asked me if I thought we should start seeing other people and I answered that it might be a good idea. We agreed we'd be the same kind of friends as we'd been before we started dating. That wasn't really saying much. A few days later when I saw her holding hands with a senior, my only thought was that I was glad it was over.

I went to Florida with the White's again at the beginning of the summer and I accused Greg of brainwashing me.

"I didn't do anything," Greg insisted. "All I did was tell you the truth!"

"Well, a fat lot of good it did me!" I snapped. "Now I can't stop thinking about Laci and she's hanging around with Tanner all the time . . ."

"Love hurts," he smiled, shaking his head.

"I'm glad that my misery is bringing you so much enjoyment," I said. "So is she dating Tanner . . . or are they just friends . . . or what?"

"That's between you and Tanner and Laci," he told me, throwing his hands into the air. "I'm minding my own business."

144

"*NOW?*" I asked, incredulous. "*NOW* you're minding your own business?"

"Yeah," he nodded. "I think I'll start now."

"Thanks a lot."

"No problem," he said. "Anything for a friend."

~ ~ ~

TANNER AND MIKE had football training camp at the high
school the week after we got back from Florida and I was waiting for
them when their practice ended on Monday. They came out of the
locker room with their hair wet and gym bags slung over their
shoulders, looking surprised to see me.

"What's up?" Mike asked.

"Nothing much," I replied.

"How was Florida?" Tanner asked.

"Hot."

I dangled my car keys in front of Mike's face.

"Hey Mikey," I said. "My car's in the lower lot. Wanna go get
it?"

"Really?" He only had a learner's permit and wasn't supposed to
drive alone.

"One scratch, Mikey . . . *one scratch* and I'm going to kill you."

"Oh relax!" he said, snatching the keys from my hand.

When he was gone I turned to Tanner.

"I wanted to talk to you for a second."

"About Laci?" he asked.

My mouth dropped open.

"I wondered what was taking you so long," he went on. "You
wanna know what's going on between us, don't you?"

I nodded dumbly at him.

"That's what I figured."

But then he didn't say anything further; he just stared at me.
Finally I broke the silence.

"*Well?*"

"Well, what?" he asked and I realized he wasn't going to make
this easy on me.

"What's going on between you and Laci?"

146

He looked at me for a moment and then gazed up at the ceiling as if he were studying it. Finally he rubbed his chin and in a Southern drawl he began.

"Well, I'm figurin' after high school we'll be gettin' married and have us a passel of young 'uns. Maybe get us a basset hound . . . name it Toby . . ."

"Come on, Tanner. Be serious."

"Why?" he smiled. "You're *so* fun to pick on."

"Because," I said, not seeing the humor. "I came here as a friend and I'm asking you as a friend. What's going on?"

"Man, nothing's going on."

"Are you sure? I need to know that you aren't serious about her."

"Even if I *was* serious about her, it wouldn't matter . . ."

"Yes it would!"

"Greg's right. You really are dense – you know that?"

"I'm *dense?*" I asked. "Then why don't you explain it to me? Spell it out in plain English."

"Okay," he said, putting a hand on each of my shoulders and looking into my eyes. "Listen to me *care-ful-ly*. I'm going to speak very *slow-ly* so maybe you can *un-der-stand*. No one knows why . . . it certainly isn't your good looks or your bubbly personality, but – for whatever reason – *Laci likes you.*

"Now Laci's not the type to sit at home and cry while she waits for you to come to your senses – she *is* going to go out with other guys and have fun. But for some reason – I don't know why and *trust me*, I've tried to figure it out – for some reason, no other guy is going to have a real shot at Laci, because she likes *you.*"

Before I could answer, Mike came bursting through the door and slid to a stop in front of us. His hair was tousled and his eyes wild.

"Oh, man, David! I'm sorry! It was an accident. I'm so sorry!"

I clapped my hands over my eyes. *My car. He'd wrecked my car.* My parents were going to ground me forever.

I took a deep breath. *It's just a car*, I told myself. *Nothing that can't be replaced. Mike's okay, that's all that matters . . .*

"What happened?" I asked quietly, holding my breath and peeking out between my fingers. He was grinning at me.

"Nothing." He turned to Tanner. "He's so easy, you know that? It's not even a challenge anymore."

"It never really was," Tanner said, clapping a hand on my shoulder. "See, Davey? I told you you're fun to pick on."

I breathed out a sigh of relief . . . not just about the car. We walked through the door together and I shook my head. "I really hate you both, you know that, right?"

"Yep," Mike said.

"We know," Tanner agreed.

Now all I had to do was talk to Laci.

~ ~ ~

I MOPED AROUND for the next couple of weeks. By the time summer was almost halfway over all I'd managed to do was to avoid Laci.

"Why don't you go over there and talk to her?" Greg asked one day. I was sitting in my lifeguard chair watching Laci as she and Ashlyn spread towels on their lounge chairs.

"Because I'm working."

"Go ahead," he said. "I'll cover for you."

"No thanks," I answered. "I don't need a lawsuit right now."

"Oh, I wouldn't let more than a couple of people drown."

"No thanks," I said again. "I'm good."

"You can't put it off forever," he persisted.

"Wanna bet?"

"You're a piece of work," he said. "You know that?"

"I know."

"Why don't you just *talk* to her?" he asked. "It's Laci! You've been talking to her your whole life!"

"I don't know what to say . . . I don't know what to do!"

"Well," he said, "what'd you do with Sam?"

"It was different with Sam."

"But at some point you actually decided to make a move or something . . . how'd you make yourself do it?"

I thought back to the first day of Life Skills before answering.

"I decided exactly what I wanted to have happen and then I made a list of things that would help me get there. Then I made myself do those things."

"So why don't you do that again?" he asked.

I looked at him uncertainly, but finally answered. "I guess I could try."

I hardly ever used my desk in the summer and it was cluttered with stuff. That night I removed everything and threw it onto my bed and I took out a clean sheet of paper and a pencil. I sat there for a long time trying to remember my Life Skills teacher's instructions about writing goals in a positive way and putting them in the present tense.

I finally gave up and just wrote her name at the top of my paper in large, capital letters.

LACI.

I traced the letters over and over again with my pencil until they were dark. Then I wrote a number one underneath it and beside that I wrote:

Talk to Laci.

I sighed. There really wasn't anything left to do. I picked up my phone and called her.

"Hi, David!" she answered.

"Hi," I replied. "What are you doing?"

"Babysitting Charlotte," she said. "Greg's working and Mr. and Mrs. White went out to see a movie."

That would have been a good segue . . . I could have just asked her if she wanted to go see a movie sometime, but instead I asked her if she'd driven or walked to Greg's house.

"I walked," she said.

"What time will they be home?"

"About nine-thirty."

"Is it okay if I meet you there and walk you home?"

There was a slight pause and then she answered, "Sure, that'd be good."

"See you then."

"Bye," she replied.

I looked at my watch . . . it was seven-thirty.

Two more hours.

I put my head on my desk and sighed, wondering what I'd just done.

I got there at nine o'clock and sat on the front steps. I had started to ring the bell but couldn't bring myself to do it. Instead I studied the thick hedges by the door that I had hidden behind when Greg and I'd had snowball fights and the white doorbell that I had helped Charlotte ring when she was little and the concrete planter that I'd chipped with a baseball when I was thirteen. I tried to forget why I was there.

Greg's parents showed up just after nine-thirty, surprised to see me.

"Hi, David," Mr. White said. "Are you waiting for Greg? I don't think he gets off work until ten."

"Um, no," I said, "I was just waiting for Laci. I'm going to walk her home."

"Oh," he said. He looked puzzled, but I saw the faintest smile cross Mrs. White's lips.

They went past me and a few minutes later Laci came out. I stood up.

"Hi," I said.

"Hi."

"Are you ready?"

She nodded.

We walked the three blocks between her house and Greg's in silence. The entire time I scolded myself for not having planned what I was going to do next and I wondered if I was a complete idiot.

We arrived at her house and stopped at the bottom of the stairs.

"Well," she said. "Thanks for walking me home." I nodded and she started to turn to head up the stairs.

"Laci, wait!" I said, grabbing at her sleeve.

She turned around and looked at me expectantly.

"I, um . . . I wanted to talk to you about something," I said, letting go of her sleeve.

"Okay."

My heart was pounding so loudly that I was sure she could hear it. I stood there looking at her until finally she asked, "What do you want to talk about?"

"I like your hair," I blurted, removing any doubt in my mind as to whether or not I was a complete idiot.

She must have been drawing the same conclusion because she looked at me quizzically.

"You . . . you like my hair?"

I tried to explain.

"Yeah, you know. I like your hair when it's at stage two – it's my favorite stage."

I couldn't believe it. I didn't think it was possible, but I was actually making things worse.

"Stage two?"

"Um, yeah. You know, stage one is right after you've cut it off, and stage two is like it is right now and uh . . ." I couldn't stop babbling, "stage three is right before you get it cut off again and–"

She tilted her face toward me and pressed her mouth against mine and I was glad to hear the sound of my own voice stop. I kissed her back and wrapped one hand around her waist and gathered up her hair with the other. When we finally pulled away from each other I kept my hand on her hair.

152

"Anyway," I said softly, stroking her hair, "this is my favorite stage."

She smiled at me and nodded. "Me too."

~ ~ ~

OUR SENIOR YEAR started a few weeks later and I was content in every way possible. Greg and I had first lunch together and usually worked on AP Physics while we ate. Laci and Tanner and Mike all had second lunch together and probably enjoyed laughing at how absurd I had been over the summer, but I didn't care.

Like the fall before, Greg and Laci and I went to every football game to cheer Tanner and Mike on, but Greg wouldn't sit with us unless we made him (which we usually did). When the weather turned cold and he saw Laci wearing the leather jacket he'd bought me, he just smiled.

"What are you going to get Laci for Christmas?" Greg asked over lunch one day after we'd closed our physics books. Christmas was only three weeks away.

"I don't know . . ." I said. I wanted to get her something special, but I had no idea just what that should be.

"More importantly," he asked, "what are you going to get *me* for Christmas?"

"I don't know," I said again, "but there's a ten-dollar limit this year . . . *understand?* I'm *not* gonna spend all next year feeling guilty about how much money you spent on me."

"I've really enjoyed my magazine . . ." he said honestly.

"I know, but I mean it. Don't you *dare* spend a lot of money on me this year . . . promise?"

"Oh, don't worry. I didn't," he said.

"You've already got me something?"

"Yup. Didn't go a penny over six dollars!"

"Good," I said. "Keep it that way."

The truth was that I'd already gotten him something too. It was the best graphing calculator that I could find. It had a backlit color screen and the same computer software applications that engineers

154

used. It probably didn't cost as much as the jacket had, but it was close and I couldn't wait to surprise him.

He loaded up his backpack and slung it over his shoulder.

"Where are you going?" I asked, looking at my watch. There were still over five minutes left in lunch.

"I forgot to give Dad something," he said. "I'll see you after school."

I waved my hand at him and he turned around to go. He'd cut his hair over the summer again and it had not yet reached stage two – he couldn't quite get it into a ponytail.

"See ya later," I said as he started to walk away.

It was the last time I ever saw him.

~ ~ ~

I WAS TRYING to get out of the lunch room before the bell rang to avoid the crowded halls. I walked up the stairs leading out of the cafeteria and started to reach for the door handle when one of the vice-principals, holding a walkie-talkie, stepped in front of me and shooed me away.

"Get down there," he ordered in a quiet voice and pointed beyond the cash registers.

I turned around, puzzled, and looked to where he was pointing. The teachers who were on lunch duty were scurrying around, herding students into the kitchen area where the food was prepared. Suddenly I realized what was going on. We were on lock-down.

I followed the teachers' orders and sat down between a huge stainless-steel refrigerator and a small group of freshmen girls who were almost hysterical. I'd been sitting there for about two minutes when my phone vibrated. It was Laci.

"Hi," I said, keeping my voice quiet. I didn't want to get my phone taken away.

"Are you okay?" she whispered. She sounded terrified.

"I'm fine . . . .are you?"

"I'm so scared . . ." she said.

"Relax," I told her. "It's probably nothing. Remember last year?" A nearby bank had been robbed and the gunman had fled 'in the direction of our school'. We'd been on lock-down for almost three hours until he was apprehended – ten miles away.

"Ashlyn heard gunshots," she whispered, and the hair on my arms stood up.

"Where?"

"Upstairs," she answered.

Second floor. Math and science.

"Where are you?" I asked.

156

"World Lit."

English Department. First floor.

I told her I'd call her back in a little bit.

I sent a text to my mom: Im ok r u?

Then I called Greg, but I didn't get any answer. I called Tanner and he told me that he and Mike were in the locker room off of the gym. I tried Greg again.

All around me students were texting and calling each other. They whispered to each other any new piece of information they learned from fellow classmates. We heard sirens outside the building. After about fifteen minutes I heard someone say the word *physics* and I sent a text to Greg: *call me!* I saw figures rushing past the cafeteria windows and I saw white letters on their black uniforms: SWAT.

After another fifteen minutes Mom answered my text: Im ok. I luv u.

Thirty minutes later Dad called.

"Are you okay, Son?"

"I'm fine, Dad. Mom said she's okay . . . did she call you?"

"No . . . I called her. I saw the news reports on TV."

"It's on TV? What are they saying?"

"They don't know much yet . . . a lone gunman, shots fired." His voice broke. "I love you, David."

"I love you too," I said. "Dad?"

"What?"

"I can't get in touch with Greg . . . he must have his phone turned off . . . can you try to call his dad?"

"I'll see what I can do."

"Thanks, Dad. I love you."

"I love you too."

Another hour went by and when I didn't hear anything I called Dad.

"Did you get in touch with Mr. White?"

"He's not answering . . ."

"I'm scared, Dad . . ."

"I know, David, I am too."

"Dad? Do you think maybe you should call Mrs. White? I don't want to get her worried or anything, but maybe she's heard something . . ."

"I'm with her right now," he said. "She hasn't heard anything."

"She's at your office?" I asked, very confused.

"No," Dad said. "We're outside . . . at your school."

My call waiting beeped and I told Dad I had to go. I answered the other call.

"Greg?"

"David?" It was Jessica.

"Oh . . . hi . . ." I said.

"Are you okay, David? Are you okay?" She was crying.

"It's okay, Jessica. I'm fine . . . Mom's fine . . ."

"I love you, David . . ."

"I love you too, Jess. I gotta go, though. I'm waiting for Greg to call."

"Okay," she said, and I hung up.

I had never used God as if He were a genie in a bottle, but I know some people do – only talking to Him when they need something, asking for favors, promising Him anything if He would only answer their prayers. It says in the Bible to thank God for everything and I'd always tried to do that. I tried to thank Him for what was happening now, but I couldn't. I *begged* Him to please let Greg and Mr. White be alright. I prayed for Him to take care of Laci and my mom and Tanner and Mike.

And I waited for Greg to call, but he never did.

~ ~ ~

IT WAS DARK by the time they finally let us out of the cafeteria. Just like I'd seen on TV, they had us put our hands on the back of our heads and rush out the door – police and SWAT team members directing an endless line of students to their waiting parents. A helicopter hovered noisily overhead and I searched the crowd for several minutes before finally spotting Mom.

"Dad's here somewhere," I said after we'd hugged.

"I know," she said. "Over here . . ." and she led me toward the entrance to the football field.

I slowed when I saw Dad because he was holding Charlotte. She was asleep in his arms and I could tell he'd been crying. I stopped walking, but Mom kept going and when she reached him they hugged. He said something to her and they both looked toward the ticket booth. I followed their gaze and saw a police officer trying to comfort a woman who was sobbing uncontrollably. I stepped closer to her, trying to make out who it was under the news camera lights. I thought I already knew, but I had to find out for sure. I spoke her name, hoping she wouldn't look up, but she did.

It was Mrs. White.

~ ~ ~

THE GUNMAN'S NAME was Kyle Dunn. He had been a year ahead of me in school and had dropped out when he was a junior. I vaguely recognized him from the yearbook picture and the mug shots that were flashed up on the TV screen during every news report.

After being holed up in Mr. White's room for hours, he had surrendered peacefully. Only two other people had been in the room with him and he had killed them both.

Their funerals were on Saturday.

~ ~ ~

MRS. WHITE SENT word through Mom, asking if I wanted to give a eulogy.

No, I didn't think I was going to be able to do that.

Did I want to be a pall bearer?

Maybe I could handle that.

Mom made me try on the suit I'd bought for the wedding last year and I was grateful that it still fit because I didn't want to go shopping for a new one.

Through it all, I didn't cry a single tear.

Mom said that Mrs. White had invited me to go to the visitation early . . . during the time when only family would be there. I took the calculator I had bought for Greg and slipped it into my pocket before I headed out the door.

When I got to the funeral home I found Mrs. White and Greg's grandmother and Charlotte near the door of the chapel and I hugged them all, but still I didn't cry. I looked past them to the front of the chapel and saw two identical white caskets. They were closed, with cascades of flowers flowing over the tops of both of them. Concerned, I touched my jacket and felt the calculator that I'd brought with me – I'd been planning on slipping it into Greg's casket.

I didn't want to upset Mrs. White by asking so I went out front and found a man wearing a badge from the funeral home.

"Why are the caskets closed?"

"One of the deceased is not suitable for viewing," he said.

"What do you mean?"

"When someone is," he hesitated, "disfigured . . . it's sometimes impossible to make them presentable for viewing. An open casket would be too upsetting for the loved ones."

I understood. One of them had been shot in the face.

161

"Which one?" I asked.

He hesitated again before answering.

"The young man."

"Thank you," I said, and I continued down the sidewalk to my car.

I drove to Greg's house and pulled alongside the curb. My new plan was to get the key they kept hidden in the garage, go into their house, and place the calculator under their Christmas tree. As soon as I got there, however, I knew I was *never* going to be able to go into their house, ever again, so I made a third plan.

The calculator was wrapped in Christmas paper and I had changed the tag so that it said: "To – Charlotte". I wasn't sure what to put after the word "From –", so I'd left it blank. I opened up their mailbox and stuck it inside. It was going to be five or six years before she was really going to need a graphing calculator at school, but – in the meantime – she could use it to pass notes to her friends.

At the funerals the next day, Tanner and Mike both gave eulogies. My dad was one of the pall bearers for Mr. White's casket. Laci and Ashlyn and Natalie and Tanner and Mike and I were pall bearers for Greg's. I hadn't known that girls could be pall bearers. Everyone was invited to a gathering with the family after the funerals and then I found out that it was going to be at Greg's house.

I didn't go.

I remembered mom telling me how she hadn't cried after her father's funeral . . . how she had finally just collapsed on the stairs and lost it. I knew that Mom was waiting for *me* to collapse on the stairs . . . break down and lose it . . . but I didn't think it was going to happen. I mostly felt numb and nauseous. I was rarely hungry, but whenever I was Mom always ran down to *Hunter's* and picked me up a giant sub, hoping I would eat.

I got a letter from State telling me that my room assignment had been finalized. It said that I was assigned to 307 Doughton Hall and that my roommate was Gregory P. White.

The weeks went by and still I didn't cry and I didn't react and I quit doing almost everything. I didn't watch TV because I never knew when a news story might pop up about the shooting or about Kyle Dunn and his trial and I really didn't want to hear it. Mike and Tanner and Laci called me a lot after the funeral, but I never answered the phone and whenever Mom told me someone was on the line, I would say that I was busy. After a while, even Laci stopped calling.

I arrived at school each day just in time to slide into my seat when the last bell rang. I sat by myself at lunch and kept busy by immersing myself in schoolwork . . . especially studying for the AP Physics exam. Other kids in the class were studying hard too – dedicating their efforts to the memory of Mr. White – but I did it because it seemed that the only time I didn't think about Greg was when I was totally wrapped up in a physics problem.

After school my car was one of the first out of the parking lot and I told Coach Covington that I needed to quit the swim team in order to concentrate on my studies. Baseball tryouts took place the last week in February, but I didn't attend.

Mom tried to get me to go "see someone".

"I don't need a shrink, Mom."

"I don't mean a shrink . . . I just mean someone that you can talk with and tell them how you're feeling."

"I'm not feeling anything."

"David, I'm worried about you . . ."

"I'm not going to cut my wrists or anything," I assured her. I'd seen a pamphlet sticking out of her purse a few weeks ago: *Teenage Depression and Suicide*. She didn't need to worry . . . I hadn't even thought about suicide. But I was well aware that everyone was extremely concerned about me. As a matter of fact, I was very aware of *everything* that was going on around me, but at the same time I was strangely detached from it all.

The week after Tanner and Mike made the varsity baseball team, the phone rang and Mom knocked on my door. I was surprised because she had quit trying to get me to take calls a long time ago.

"It's for you," Mom said.

"I'm busy."

She didn't say anything, but she held the phone in front of my face. I pushed my book aside and took it from her. She didn't close the door until she'd heard me say "Hello?"

"David?" I didn't recognize her voice at first.

"Yes?"

"It's Dana."

That threw me for a second too, because I had always called her Mrs. White.

"Yes?" I said, sitting up on the bed, my heart beginning to pound wildly.

164

"I need you to come over for a few minutes," she said.

Her call and her request caught me so off guard that I couldn't even think of anything to say. My first thought was that she needed me to watch Charlotte for her.

"David?"

"You want me to come over now?"

"Yes, now. It won't take very long."

"I'll be right there," I said, and she hung up the phone without saying goodbye. I turned the phone off and stared at it for a long while. Then I grabbed my leather jacket and headed out the door.

"You're not *driving* over there, are you?" Mom asked when she saw me taking my keys.

"I'll be fine."

"It's getting icy," she said. I kept walking.

"I think a walk in the fresh air would do you good . . ." she called after me.

"I'll be fine," I repeated, and I jumped into my car and slammed the door.

The roads *were* getting icy – especially on the other side of town where I somehow wound up. I hadn't been able to bring myself to make the right-hand turn at the end of my block that would take me to Greg's house, and by the time my car fishtailed and almost hit a phone pole I had been driving aimlessly for almost an hour. My phone rang, but I ignored it and headed back in the direction of Greg's.

As I pulled into the driveway my phone went off for a second time and I answered it only because I knew that it was Mom again and that she was worried sick.

"I'm fine," I said before she could say a word.

"Where are you?"

"I'm here. I just got here. I'm fine."

"David . . ."

"I gotta go," I said, hanging up as I turned off the car.

I couldn't even *look* at his house, so instead I gripped the steering wheel and rested my head against it, trying to figure out how I was going to manage to walk up to the door and ring that bell.

I'm not sure how long I sat there like that or when I knew that Mrs. White was standing outside the car, but even before she laid her hand on the shoulder of my leather jacket and even before she opened my door and spoke my name, somehow I knew she was there.

That's when I finally lost it.

I remember sobbing uncontrollably, my shoulders shaking up and down, and several months' worth of tears spilling out of my eyes. I remember thinking that I didn't want to be there and I didn't want Mrs. White to see me crying and that I was going to ruin my jacket if I didn't stop.

Somehow she got me inside and onto the couch and she sat there for a long time with her arms around me while I cried. I kept apologizing for crying and she kept telling me that it was okay and she gave me a clean dish towel for my face and my jacket.

I finally asked her where Charlotte was because I was still thinking that she needed me to watch her. Mrs. White told me that Charlotte was spending the night at a friend's house, and that's when

I realized that she and my mother had been conspiring against me (or maybe for me) and that sitting on that couch, crying my eyes out, was exactly where they had both wanted me to be.

I woke up in the morning on the couch, still in my jacket, with an afghan tucked around me and the smell of coffee brewing in the kitchen. Mrs. White made me take off my jacket and eat breakfast, but I really just wanted to get out of there.

"I have something for you before you go," she said after I'd managed to eat. She handed me a small package wrapped in green foil paper.

I took it from her and looked at the "Merry Christmas" tag. I recognized the handwriting before I read the words.

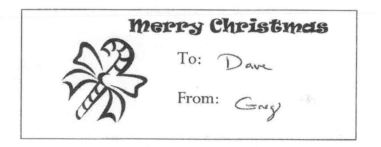

I had one more jag of crying before I put my jacket back on and left. Considering everything that it had been through, it didn't look too bad.

~ ~ ~

AFTER MY BREAK down (or break through) at Greg's house, I started returning each weekend to help shovel snow or cut dangerous tree limbs or salt the walks. After spring turned into summer, I could often be found there, mowing the lawn, pulling weeds, or trimming hedges. Laci started showing up a lot too, helping Mrs. White with Charlotte.

Sometimes, after Charlotte was in bed, I would find myself in the living room with Mrs. White and Laci. Those were the only times when I would allow myself to feel anything or let someone else see into my heart. They were the only times I knew for sure that I was still alive. The moment I left Greg's house, I would turn my feelings back off and shut everybody back out.

I did so well on the AP Physics exam that I went off to State in September with six semester hours of college credit. My roommate was named Todd and he was from Texas. I felt bad for him because I could tell he really wanted me to be a friend, but it just wasn't going to happen. It wasn't because he was sleeping on what should have been Greg's bed each night or studying at what should have been Greg's desk. Mostly, it was because I was detached from everything that was going on around me, except for the times when I was at Greg's house with Laci and Mrs. White.

Laci went to Collens, which was on the other side of Cavendish and about four hours away from State, but we were both close enough to Cavendish that we returned home almost every weekend. Invariably, we wound up together at Greg's house over and over again.

"Are you coming to church tomorrow?" Laci asked as I was walking her home one evening.

It was a stupid question and she knew it. I hadn't been to church since the funeral.

"Probably not," I said, continuing to pace along.

"You know," she said, stopping on the sidewalk and grabbing my arm so that I stopped too, "you can't stay mad at God forever."

"You think that's why I haven't been going to church?" I asked her, almost laughing and shaking my head. "I'm not mad at God."

She looked slightly relieved, but she still persisted.

"Why then?"

I shrugged and started walking again so that she had no choice but to come along.

"I don't really want to talk about it, Laci," I said, and I was glad when she let it drop.

The truth was that when I wasn't at Greg's house I removed myself as far from God as I did from everyone else.

One night I was working on a calculus problem when Todd interrupted me. He was examining something small and shiny. It was probably a coin, but I didn't ask.

"Do you have a magnifying glass?" he asked.

I did. It was in my top desk drawer, rewrapped loosely in the green foil with the "Merry Christmas" tag still on it.

"No," I lied, "sorry."

I'd waited about three weeks to unwrap it after Mrs. White had given it to me. The night I finally opened it I lay in bed, puzzling over why Greg had bought it for me. Suddenly I got it.

Sam and I were so far apart that I had needed a telescope to see her, but Laci and I were so close . . .

Maybe Greg had been right, maybe Laci had been *'the one'*. Before he'd been killed, it had certainly seemed as if Laci and I were headed that way. But ever since Greg and Mr. White had died, I'd regarded Laci the same way I did Mrs. White – she was someone to remember them with . . . someone to grieve with – nothing more.

Walking her home another night she stopped me again.

"I'm worried about you, David."

"I'm fine," I said, for what seemed like the millionth time.

"You're not fine," she argued. "You aren't enjoying life – you're barely even living!"

I started walking again and she had to hustle to catch up.

"Do you think you're the only one who misses him?" she shouted, tugging at my arm. "Look at Mrs. White! Do you see *her* shutting everybody else out? Do you see *her* feeling sorry for herself all the time?"

I knew it ticked her off that the only time I let her in was when I was at Greg's house. She was trying to make me mad . . . anything to get a rise out of me.

"Greg wouldn't want this," she said, softly. "He'd want you to be happy."

She was looking for some emotion – *any emotion* – good or bad.

She shouldn't have wasted her time.

"I don't want to be happy," I told her, and I kept on walking.

"Laci's worried about you," Mrs. White told me the next weekend.

"I know," I said, "but she doesn't need to be."

"Greg always thought that you and Laci would be together," she said. "You know that, right?"

170

I couldn't help but laugh. "He might have mentioned it a few hundred times."

She smiled.

"Laci's a sweet girl."

I nodded.

"She cares about you."

"I know," I said, nodding again. "I care about her too."

"No, you don't," she said, reaching over and laying her hand on mine. "You don't care about anything anymore."

I knew I'd be lying to her if I tried to argue.

The following weekend we spent the afternoon at Greg's, raking leaves into piles for Charlotte to jump into. As usual, I walked Laci home.

"Good night," she said, heading up the stairs to her front door.

"Laci?"

She was at the top of the stairs. She let go of the door handle and turned back around.

"What?"

"I want to ask you something," I said, "and I want you to tell me the truth."

"Okay."

I held up my hand in the circle that Greg had always signaled her with.

"What does this mean?"

She stared at me for a long time before answering.

"He'll come around."

I looked at her, not quite sure what she meant, but almost.

"He was telling me to give you time . . . that one day you'd come around . . . that you'd like me back . . ."

I dropped my eyes and looked at the ground, thinking about the first time I'd seen him give her that signal.

We had been in the seventh grade.

"I'm sorry, Laci," I finally said, looking back up at her. "I'm really sorry."

"I know," she said, and I turned around and walked home.

~ ~ ~

ON THE ANNIVERSARY of Greg and Mr. White's death, I arrived to help Mrs. White and Charlotte and Laci decorate for Christmas. The lights were already on the tree and we began unpacking ornaments. The second one I opened was a little felt reindeer. On the back was a piece of masking tape with the name "Greg" written on it. I handed it to Laci and took Charlotte outside to put lights on the big spruce tree near the edge of the yard.

"David?" Charlotte asked.

"What, Charlotte?"

"Do you think it'll snow?"

I looked up through the cold air into the magnificent black sky with thousands of brilliant stars. Asterisms and constellations.

"Not tonight."

"Maybe by Christmas?" she asked.

"Maybe."

"David?"

"What?"

"Did you give me that calculator last year?"

I nodded at her.

"Did you buy it for Greg?"

I nodded again.

"I miss him," she said.

"I know, Charlotte. I miss him too. And your dad."

"I like the calculator though."

"Good."

"My mom says you're having a hard time."

I didn't say anything.

"She says we have to pray for you every day. I pray for you a lot." She paused. "Is it helping?"

"I'm sure it is," I said, kneeling down next to her.

"Do you want me to keep praying for you?"

"Yes, please," I said, hugging her so she wouldn't see my tears. She rested her head on my shoulder.

"Do you know what, David?"

"What?"

"Jordan threw up at school yesterday."

"Oh!" I said, standing up. "That must have been interesting."

"It was gross. Mrs. Germaine had to call the janitor and we got to go outside on the playground until he cleaned it up."

"Well, that sounds like fun."

"It was okay," she said, shrugging. "We couldn't get out any of the jump-ropes or four-square balls though so the only thing we got to do was play on the monkey bars."

I let her rattle on until I was sure the tree inside was done.

~ ~ ~

LEARNING THAT AN eight-year old little girl was praying for me every day woke something up inside of me. If I had put one moment's worth of thought into it earlier, I would have realized that *many* people were praying for me, but I hadn't. Maybe Laci had been right – I'd been too busy feeling sorry for myself.

I returned to college and began waking up even more. Todd was surprised when I accepted his offer one night to go get pizza. I talked with the head swim coach about joining the team . . . not right now, but maybe next year? I told him my times and he nodded. We could probably work something out.

I signed up for summer classes and trained at the college pool all summer. I went for long runs and pumped weights and joined a local church that had a huge population of college students. I began to make new friends.

At the same time though, I quit going home to Cavendish. It seemed as if there was a limit as to how much I was going to be able to open up and let others in, and something had to go. I called Tanner and Mike and asked them to check in on Mrs. White from time to time. Tanner said that he would. Mike said he would too, but that the last time he'd gone to church, he'd heard that Mrs. White was dating one of the deacons who was a widower. I got a letter from Charlotte. She said that Mr. Barnett had taken her and her mom to Six Flags.

In the fall of my sophomore year, Jessica and her husband came to visit me at State. She wanted to tell me in person . . . I was going to be an uncle. We tromped around the campus, talking of her old times there and my new ones. Her husband waited in the car while we said goodbye.

"I'm so glad you're doing okay," she said softly, and I smiled at her. She looked at me with tears in her eyes. "We were all so worried about you."

"Don't worry about *me*," I said, patting her stomach. "I'm fine."

This time I meant it.

~ ~ ~

THE NEXT SUMMER I had to officially declare my major and I chose engineering. I was certain by now that I was doing it for the right reasons. I thoroughly enjoyed the classes and I was doing very well – I'd made the dean's list every semester.

I remembered what Mom had said about some people not knowing what they wanted to do until years after they graduated and I understood that God was going to guide my steps if I just listened to Him. I'd been doing that, too.

I used that same understanding during the fall semester of my senior year. I was already getting job interviews and even a few offers from companies across the country. I didn't accept even the most attractive ones because I didn't hear God telling me what to do yet, so I just waited.

On a crisp Saturday in October I attended a football game with some friends. We were in a restaurant, celebrating afterwards, when I felt my phone vibrating. I stood up quickly, rushing to get away from the noise so that I'd be able to hear when I answered it.

"Hello?"

"David?"

"Yes?"

"This is Dana White."

"Hi!" I said, very surprised, but pleased too. "How are you?"

"I'm fine. How are you?"

"Good," I said, pausing. "Is everything alright?"

"Oh, yes," she said. "Am I catching you at a bad time?"

"No," I said. "Not at all."

"I watched the game on TV. Were you there?"

"Yeah . . ."

"Did you have fun?" she asked.

"Yeah. It was a good game."

"Yes, it was," she said. "I'm glad you had a good time.

"Listen, David," she continued. "I saw your mom at church last week. She said you're coming home for fall break?"

"Yes, I am."

"If you have any time, do you think you could swing by the house for a few minutes?"

"Sure I could," I replied. "I'm sorry I haven't been visiting much."

"I'm glad you're moving on, David. You didn't think I wanted you here mowing my lawn every weekend, did you?" I could hear laughter in her voice.

"I'll see you in a couple of weeks," I said.

"Good-bye."

"Bye."

I walked back to the table smiling. I had a feeling I knew why she wanted to see me. Through Mom and Mike I'd heard the rumors that things between her and Mr. Barnett were looking serious . . . I bet they were planning on getting married.

She probably wanted to tell me the good news herself.

The day after I got home for fall break I walked to the White's and rang the bell. Charlotte answered the door and I was taken aback by how tall she was . . . the top of her head almost reached my chin when she hugged me. She steered me into the living room and pointed to the couch.

"Mom'll be here in a minute," she said. "I'm going over to Lydia's house."

"See you later . . ." I said, raising a hand to wave goodbye.

"Oh . . . and David?"

I looked at her.

"I still have the calculator."

178

I smiled.

"Did you know you can write notes on it to your friends and the teacher thinks you're doing work?"

"Yeah," I said, wryly. "*Most* of the time. Be careful though, teachers aren't always as dumb as you might think."

Mrs. White had walked into the room.

"Young lady," she said. "You are at school to get an education, not to socialize! Do you understand me?"

"Yes, ma'am," she said, rolling her eyes at me before darting out of the room.

"How are you?" I asked, standing up to hug Mrs. White.

"I'm good," she replied. "How are you?"

"Good," I answered back, smiling.

"How's that niece of yours?" she asked.

"Spoiled rotten," I said. "She's growing so fast. Charlotte is too – I can't believe how tall she is!"

"I know," she said, shaking her head. "Sometimes I worry that she's got her priorities all mixed up though. Passing notes on a calculator . . ."

"She's only ten –"

"Eleven!" Mrs. White corrected me.

"Eleven," I said. "Anyway . . . I use to do the same stuff when I was her age. Look how great I turned out!"

"Maybe there's hope," she said, smiling. "Have a seat."

We sat on the couch.

"I wanted to talk to you about something," she began.

I nodded. Mom couldn't say enough good things about Mr. Barnett. I was happy for them both.

"I've been seeing Kyle," she began. I nodded again, but the wheels were turning in my mind. I'd thought Mr. Barnett's name was Erik.

"Have you been keeping up with his case?" I shook my head and realized she was talking about Kyle Dunn.

"Well, you know he's been on death row for over two years now?"

I nodded dumbly.

"Anyway," she continued. "His execution date has finally been set for April. I don't think there will be any more appeals . . . he's asked his lawyers not to do anything to delay it.

"He's changed a lot since he was found guilty," she continued. "A group of us from the church have been visiting him . . . praying for him . . ."

I nodded again.

"Anyway," she said. "He wants to see you."

I couldn't have been any more shocked if she had told me he was an alien.

"What?"

"He wants to see you . . . to talk to you. I thought that if you were home for Christmas break you could go by and visit him."

I was already shaking my head.

"David," she said. "You have to forgive him. As Christians, we're called to—"

"No, that's not it," I interrupted her. "I've forgiven him . . . you don't have to worry about that . . ."

The truth was that I had barely thought of Kyle at all.

"David," she said, looking into my eyes and laying a hand on mine. "Have I ever asked you to do *anything* for me?"

I shook my head at her.

"I'm asking you now. I want you to please go see Kyle over your Christmas break. Will you do that? Will you do that for me . . . *please?*"

I waited for a long moment and then I finally nodded.

"Promise me," she said.

I nodded again.

"I need to hear you say it."

"I promise," I said.

180

"Promise what?"

"I promise I'll go see Kyle . . ."

She looked at me, wanting me to say more, but I just stared at her.

"Over Christmas break?"

I nodded again.

"Say it," she said. "Over Christmas break."

I nodded one more time and answered. "Over Christmas break."

~ ~ ~

AS SOON AS I got back to school I received a message from Mrs. White:

Visitation days are every Tuesday and Thursday between 9 and 11a.m. Your name is already on the list of visitors, but you'll need to call ahead and tell them what day and time you are coming.

I called and told them I'd be there on the second Tuesday in January – the last day before I was to report back to campus for spring semester.

I spent the rest of the semester getting ready to visit Kyle. I had a feeling from what Mrs. White had said that he'd already accepted Christ, but I wasn't going to take any chances. For the first time since I'd been at college, I didn't make the dean's list – I barely made it through exams. It was a good thing that I already had a few job offers under my belt.

I went to the Christian book store and looked through all of the evangelistic books that they had, unable to find anything useful.

"Do you have anything else?" I asked the clerk.

"Would you like me to look on the computer?"

"Yes, please."

"Here are two . . . *Effective Witnessing For Every Situation* and *Prison Ministry*. Do you want me to order them?"

"How long will they take?"

182

"A few days."

"Yes, please."

I pored through my concordance and Bible, jotting down Scriptures to memorize. I told my Bible study group what I was doing and they offered to help. They thought up every scenario that might arise and coached me how to handle each one. What would I do if he was belligerent? What if he was unremorseful? What if he didn't believe he could be forgiven?

I went to the library and pulled up a copy of the *Cavendish Times* from the week after Greg and Mr. White had been killed. I paid ten cents for a hard copy and taped Kyle's mug shot photo inside the cover of my Bible. I practiced talking to it every day. I did everything I could think of to get prepared.

By the time I went home for Christmas break, I thought I was ready to go.

~ ~ ~

A WEEK AFTER New Year's I parked in the visitor's parking lot at the correctional unit and walked to the guard house. The door buzzed and I pulled it open. When it clanged closed behind me I was handed a pen and told to sign in. I wrote my name, the name of the prisoner I was there to visit, and then the date and time. I gave them my driver's license and a guard scanned a visitor's ID bracelet which she then clamped on my wrist. Another guard ran a metal detector wand all over my body and patted me down. Then I was buzzed out a second door and found myself outdoors again, within the razor wire fences of the prison compound.

I followed the sidewalk to a large brick building and was buzzed in again. I entered a spacious lobby. Idly, I noticed how clean everything looked. A man in a drab, gray prison uniform pushed a dust mop back and forth and I read the number on his shirt: 73958.

There were five doors leading off of the lobby and a large dark window overseeing them all. I could just make out shadowy figures beyond the glass. I looked at each door.

Two were bathrooms: *Men. Women.*

One door read: *Administrative Offices.*

Another: *Visitation.*

The final door read: *Authorized Personnel Only.*

I went to the one that said "Men" and I stayed in there for a long, long time. I washed my hands and then I dried them off. Then I washed my face and I dried it off too. Finally I stood with my back against the wall and rested my hands on my knees. I looked at my watch and saw that only a half of an hour remained during visitation hours. I rubbed my eyes, took a deep breath, and went back out into the lobby.

Once I was buzzed through the "Visitation" door my visitor ID bracelet was scanned again. A copy of my driver's license appeared on a computer screen and a guard looked back and forth between my picture and my face. She looked at her watch, pecked at a few keys, and then pushed a button.

"Kyle Dunn," she said into a microphone. She nodded to her right and I was buzzed through yet another door.

A guard was in the small room that I entered. He pulled out a chair and nodded at me.

"Have a seat," he said. The guard stood behind me and I sat down, facing the Plexi-glass partition, and looked at the empty chair on the other side of it. There was a phone on each side of the partition. I folded my hands in my lap, looked at them, and waited.

I sat there, staring at my hands, until the guard spoke to me.

"Sir?" he said.

I looked back at him. "Yes?"

The guard nodded toward the Plexi-glass and I looked at it – through it – to see Kyle Dunn, sitting in the chair that was opposite me, holding the phone to his ear.

~ ~ ~

THE CORRECTIONAL FACILITY was in the middle of nowhere and I had no phone reception when I got back to my car. I had to drive for ten minutes until I could get a decent signal. I hadn't called Laci in over three years, but I knew her number by heart.

All I got was her voicemail. I hung up and threw the phone to the other side of the car. A piece of its plastic housing flew into the air and the phone landed on the floorboard.

I banged my palm on the steering wheel and drove faster. I was ten minutes from Laci's house when my phone rang which surprised me because I was sure I'd broken it. I somehow managed to lean down and grab it without wrecking the car. I answered it, pulling over to the side of the road as I did.

"David?"

I didn't say anything.

"David? Are you there? David?"

"I'm here."

"Did you try to call me?"

"Yeah. I'm sorry . . . I shouldn't have called you. I'm sorry."

"What's the matter, David?"

"I don't know . . . look, I just . . . I don't know . . . *oh, my God, Laci . . . I really screwed up . . .*"

"David . . . calm down. Talk to me. What's going on?"

"I went to see Kyle . . ." I said, starting to cry. "I need to see you, Laci. I'm sorry to bother you, but I think I need to see you."

"Where are you?"

"I'm almost to your house."

"I'm not at my house," she said. "I'm on campus."

"Laci . . . I'm sorry." I said, still crying. "I don't know what to do."

"David, listen to me," she said. "I want you to go to Cross Lake, okay? I'll meet you there."

"I'm sorry," I said again.

"Please be careful."

Fifty minutes later I pulled into the parking lot at Cross Lake Marina. I got out and paced around the picnic table where we had once played cards. When Laci pulled up I sat down. She got out of her car and sat next to me, putting her hand on my shoulder.

"I went to see Kyle," I began.

"I know."

"I really do forgive him . . ." I said, glancing at her. She nodded.

"And, I really do want him to be saved . . . and I wanted to have a part in that, but . . ."

"But, what?" she asked softly when I hesitated.

"But I don't think that's the only reason I went."

"What do you mean?"

I sat there quietly for a long moment, trying to figure out how to put it into words.

Finally I said, "If Kyle *is* saved, if he goes to Heaven . . ."

My voice broke and I had to pause again.

"If he goes to Heaven . . . then he's going to get to see Greg," I whispered and tears filled my eyes.

"I wanted to do such a good job when I talked to Kyle because I thought Greg might ask him about me . . ." I was crying again. "I wanted Greg to be proud of me and I wanted to let him know that I was still running a good race and that I was going to see him again."

"What happened?" Laci asked me quietly.

"He asked me what this meant," I said, and I twisted my index finger into my palm.

"What did you tell him?"

"I didn't tell him anything!" I cried. "I was so shocked . . . I just lost it! I completely lost it! I jumped up and my chair fell over and I was yelling at him and I told him he had no right to ever do that and I ran out of there as soon as the guard could get the door open.

"I thought I was prepared for anything . . . I'd worked so hard and I wanted to do so good. But when he asked me that I . . . I just couldn't believe it!" I wiped my eyes and took a deep breath. "I screwed up so bad, Laci. I don't know what to do."

She took her hand off of my shoulder and paused for a long moment before she spoke.

"This is my fault," she finally said.

"What are you talking about?"

"I should have . . . I should have warned you. I knew he was probably going to ask you about that and I should have told you. I'm sorry."

I looked at her, bewildered.

"How could you *possibly* have known he was going to ask me about it?"

"Because he asked *me* what it meant and I told him it was something between you and me and Greg and that I didn't know if I could tell him or not. I told him that he needed to ask you."

"When did you talk to him?"

"I've been visiting him . . ." she said.

I rubbed my forehead.

"How did he even know about it in the first place?"

"Listen, David," she said, shaking her head. "I'm not sure you really want to hear about this right now."

"Yes, I do," I insisted. "How did he know about it?"

She took a deep breath, put her fingertips together in front of her and stared at them.

"The day he killed Greg and Mr. White," she finally began, still staring at her hands, "Kyle was going to kill himself. He went to school with a gun under his jacket, and he went up to the second

188

floor. Mr. White's room was empty and Kyle went in there. He walked back to Mr. White's office. Mr. White was sitting at his desk. Kyle said he doesn't think Mr. White ever even knew he was there. I don't think even Kyle knows why, but he shot Mr. White two times and then he heard Greg yell, 'Dad!' and Kyle turned around and shot Greg too.

"Greg . . ." she hesitated. "Greg was shot in . . ." She shook her head and glanced at me. "Look, David. I really don't think you need to hear this."

"Greg was shot in the face," I said. "I know. Keep going."

She swallowed hard, looked back at her hands and nodded. "Greg was shot in the face, but he didn't . . . he didn't die right away. Kyle said that Greg kept trying to say something, but that he couldn't because . . . because of his injuries. For some reason, Kyle panicked. He got down next to Greg and asked him what he was trying to say. Greg kept trying to talk, but he couldn't, and Kyle kept asking him what he was saying.

"And then," she said, her eyes filling up with tears, "Greg did this."

She twisted her finger into her palm.

"Kyle said he quit trying to talk . . . he just kept doing it over and over until he died."

She didn't say anything for a long moment.

"I should have told you," Laci finally said. "I should have called you and told you. I'm sorry. It's my fault."

"No . . ." I said, standing up. "It's my fault, Laci. I pushed you away a long time ago. It's not your fault."

She stood up too and I took her hand.

"Thank you for coming here . . ." I said and she nodded.

I dropped her hand, walked back to my car, and drove away.

~ ~ ~

I SHOWED UP for my first day of classes on Thursday and told all of my professors that I would not be in class on the following Tuesday. I wasn't asking their permission . . . I just wanted to let them know.

~ ~ ~

ON TUESDAY MORNING I was in the visitation room just after nine o'clock and I was watching for Kyle when a guard brought him in and he sat down. He looked scared . . . as if he were really glad there was Plexi-glass between us. I picked up my phone and nodded at him, indicating for him to do the same.

"I'm sorry about last week," I said before he could say a word. He nodded.

"I shouldn't have acted the way I did. I'm ready to tell you about it now if you still want to know." He nodded again.

I started at the beginning. I told him all about Greg and Laci and their haircuts and *chop, chop* and chuffers and Mexico and sharks and telescopes and index fingers twisting into palms and then I asked him if I could pray with him and he said that I could, so I did. I left when the guard told me it was time to go and I drove to the spot where I knew I'd get a signal and I called Laci.

"David?"

"I just saw Kyle again."

"Are you alright?"

"Do you have any classes today?" I was sure that she did.

"I can meet you at Cross Lake in an hour," she offered.

"Drive careful."

~ ~ ~

I DIDN'T DRIVE as fast as I had a week earlier and she was waiting for me when I got there . . . standing next to me by the time I got out of my car.

I opened my arms and she stepped into them, laying her head against my jacket and wrapping her arms around me. I rested my cheek on the top of her head and held her tight.

We didn't say anything for a long, long time, but I knew.

I began stroking her long hair, twisting locks of it around my fingers and gathering it into my hand. Finally I buried my face into her hair, my mouth near her ear.

"Why?" I whispered. "Why do you love me?"

"God told me to," she said softly. "He told me that you were the one."

"When?"

"In preschool – when you freaked out just because I got my hair cut."

I pulled back from her and looked to see if she was serious.

She was.

"I don't think I freaked out . . ."

"Yes, you did," she argued.

"Ever since *preschool*?" I asked.

"Well, that was the first time. He had to keep reminding me over the years because you were so uncooperative."

"Are you seeing anyone?" I knew the answer, but thought I should ask anyway. She shook her head.

"What's the matter? Can't you get any guys to follow you down to Mexico City?"

Her mouth fell open. "How'd you know I was going to Mexico City?"

192

"Laci," I said, "I've known you were going to Mexico City since the day Mercedes gave you that necklace."

I kept stroking her hair and she smiled at me.

"What if there *was* some guy who wanted to follow you down to Mexico?" I asked. "How would you feel about that?"

"I'm not sure," she said. "I guess it would depend on who the guy was . . ."

"Well, what if he was an *engineer?* What if an engineer wanted to follow you down there?"

"I don't know . . ." she said. "Is he a *grumpy* engineer?"

"Sometimes."

"Only sometimes?"

"Well . . . most of the time."

"I think I'd like that," she nodded and I smiled before I answered her back.

"Me too."

~ ~ ~

KYLE IS ALLOWED to address the two witness parties. He talks to his mother and sister first. He tells them that he loves them.

He looks to me and Laci and Mrs. White next.

"Thank you for everything you've done for me. Thank you for helping me to find peace. I pray that you'll have peace, too."

He looks at Mrs. White and then Laci and they both nod at him; then he looks to me.

I think about twisting my index finger into my palm, but I don't – his wrists are strapped down and I know he won't be able to do it back. Instead I hold up two fingers to him in a "V", the universal sign for peace. He looks at them and a small smile crosses his face. He extends two fingers and does it back. The guard pulls a hood over Kyle's head and he can't see me anymore, so I turn away and look toward Laci.

She is hugging Mrs. White and they are both crying. I can only see the back of her head. Her hair is short . . . stage one.

I look down at my fingers . . . still in the peace sign. I slowly bring them together, opening and closing them like scissors.

Chop, chop.

Peace.

Can just one family make a difference? Can just one person change lives for all eternity? Be sure to read the rest of the books in the *Chop, Chop* series to discover the full impact of Greg and his family in the years that follow.

Book One: *Chop, Chop*
Book Two: *Day-Day*
Book Three: *Pon-Pon*
Book Four: *The Other Brother*
Book Five: *The Other Mothers*
Book Six: *Gone*
Book Seven: *Not Quickly Broken*
Book Eight: *Alone*

On Facebook? Please be sure to become a fan of the *Chop, Chop* page to keep up with the latest!

For more information and free downloadable lesson plans, be sure to visit: www.LNCronk.com

Ordering five or more copies of any of the *Chop, Chop* books? Save 50% off the retail price **and receive free shipping!**

For details, please visit www.LNCronk.com or send an email to: info@LNCronk.com.

While the concept of forgiveness is appreciated by people from religions and nations throughout the world, the reality that Jesus Christ loved us enough to die for the forgiveness of our sins is not. If you enjoyed *Chop, Chop* and feel others would benefit from its important message, please consider doing one or more of the following:

✂ Word of mouth is one of the most powerful tools you have available . . . ***tell others about it!***

✂ Give *Chop, Chop* as a gift.

✂ Make sure your local library has a copy of *Chop, Chop*. If they don't, ask them to order a copy for their patrons.

✂ Write a book review for your local paper, favorite magazine, or websites such as www.goodreads.com or www.Amazon.com.

✂ If you know someone in the media (newspaper, radio, TV or Internet) tell them about *Chop, Chop* and ask them to read and review it.

✂ Visit www.LNCronk.com for details on how to request a free set of *Chop, Chop* bookmarks to help spread the word.

✂ Consider donating one or more copies of *Chop, Chop* to your church library or school library.

✂ If you have a website, post a link to www.LNCronk.com.

✂ *Chop, Chop* is excellent for Sunday schools, Bible studies, home schools and other types of Christian education. Leaders can find free, downloadable lessons (many of which are stand-alone lessons that are not dependent upon the novel) at www.LNCronk.com.

✂ Order multiple copies of *Chop, Chop* at 50% off the list price for educational purposes or for resale and receive free shipping. For details, visit the website or send an email to: info@LNCronk.com.

196

Made in the USA
Charleston, SC
11 September 2014